"With realistic dialogue and characters, and brilliant, compelling writing, this is a story that should be in every secondary school library."

Emma Finlayson-Palmer, author of Autumn Moonbeam

"This debut by Kate S. Martin is magnificent! It should be required reading for all students. The prose is beautiful and the overall message is something both children and adults can learn from."

Diane Billas, author of Does Love Always Win?

"Contemporary, gritty YA is very much my jam and this was a perfect example of why I love the genre."

Louise Finch, author of The Eternal Return of Clara Hart

"Elliot and Josh's voices are distinct, compelling and surprisingly funny, and the reader winds up rooting for both of them."

Aislinn O'Loughlin, author of Big Bad Me

"Covering tricky topics such as being a young carer, domestic abuse and mental health issues, this is a beautifully written, sensitive debut full of humour, compassion and heart."

Hayley Hoskins, author of The Whisperling

"Exploring tough themes like bullying and mental illness with sensitivity and skill, it's a coming-of-age tale that stays with you long after the final page."

Lucy Brandt, author of Leonora Bolt series

"The book isn't just entertaining but also desperately important."

H. A. Robinson, author of The Pebble Jar

"An uplifting tale of self-realisation and growth."

Nick Wilford, author of The Becalmer

ALSO BY KATE S. MARTIN

Are You Okay, Elliot Hart?

Anthologies

Dark and Stormy Night- Damaged

WHAT ABOUT YOU, JOSH MCBRIDE?

KATE S. MARTIN

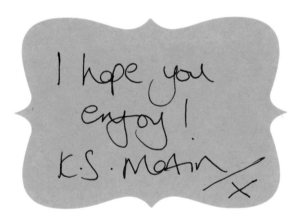

I hope you
enjoy !
K.S. Martin
x

British biscuit guide

The hobnob - a crumbly biscuit with an oaty flavour.

The chocolate digestive - a plain biscuit with one side covered in chocolate.

The custard cream - a vanilla/custard flavoured biscuit with a cream filling.

The bourbon biscuit - a chocolate flavoured biscuit with chocolate icing filling.

The jammie dodger - two vanilla biscuits with strawberry jam sandwiched in the middle.

For all my overseas readers, I didn't realize how many biscuits make it into my stories and there was some confusion when a character tucked into a Bourbon in my first book. So, here is a handy guide to British biscuits! Hope it helps.

Published in the United States by Creative James Media.

WHAT ABOUT YOU, JOSH MCBRIDE?. Copyright © 2023 by Kate Martin. All rights reserved. Printed in the United States of America. For information, address Creative James Media, 9150 Fort Smallwood Road, Pasadena, MD 21122.

www.creativejamesmedia.com

978-1-956183-74-0 (trade paperback)

First U.S. Edition 2023

To teenagers everywhere, especially those whose brains work a bit differently to the rest.

To Grandma, I love you and I miss you.

CHAPTER ONE
JOSH

Ninety-one days. Ninety-one days and then I can escape this hell-hole. A poster about the end of year prom has been stuck to Marshall's door. We get to escape this prison in three whole months! Lewis stands off to the side of the hallway, glancing in my direction. I don't know what he does with his days anymore. I started my time at St. Cuthbert's High School with him glued to my side, picking out weird kids to bully and now I'm finishing it with one of those weird kids being my half-brother.

"Come on in, year eleven. I've a surprise for you!" Marshall appears in the doorway, his black moustache shaking with excitement. I've promised Mum I'll try and pass my exams and get to college, do a joinery course Mr Hogg's told me about. Turns out, at long last, they've discovered a talent!

I can cut up wood.

Students tumble through the door, and I wait at the back, avoiding Lewis's gaze. There's something different as I stroll into the classroom, not only does Marshall look like he's had too many coffees with his breakfast, but in front of every chair are two sheets of lined paper. Nothing he finds *this* exciting can be any good. "Don't get your exercise books out but do make sure you've remembered a pen *and* your brain!" He laughs at his own joke and my jaw tenses. "Come on!" he continues. "Sit down and no peeking!" He waggles one of his hairy fingers and I want to grab it and snap it clean off. This looks suspiciously like we've a test, a test he's definitely failed to mention. I would've remembered because I want to throw up in my mouth every time a teacher mentions words like, test, exam, or assessment. It's always been this way, but ever since Elliot and I got back from our bio-father adventure, I promised Mum things would be different. No more shirking my responsibilities at school. And I meant it, even if my nerves around tests have only gotten worse.

I make my way to the front of the room and take my seat next to Highlighter Girl, who's already frantically rooting in her fluffy pencil case to choose what highlighters she might use during this lesson. Will it be putrid pink or vomit green? I feel a bit green actually, maybe I need to leave immediately and see Mrs Rogerson, the school nurse. Headache? Sudden onset of nausea? Allergic to moustached teachers and surprise assessments?

"I'll take the register and then explain what fun I've in store for you." *For someone who's supposed to be an expert on words, I think we need to define the word fun, Sir.*

This is *not* fun.

Teasing my little sisters? Making my mum jump by shouting SPIDER? *That's* fun. This is ... *hell*. This is hell wrapped up with an over excited English teacher and his surprise announcement.

A scrunched-up piece of paper flies through the air and hits the top of Edward Burns's head. "Lewis!" Marshall barks. "Pick that up!"

After the register's taken, Marshall places his Top Teacher mug onto his desk and stands at the front of the room, his arms outstretched like he's about to conduct the junior choir. "It goes without saying that these final few months are important." Here we go! The speech every teacher has tortured us with since the start of the summer term. I'll sit back and wait patiently for phrases like *do yourself proud* and *show us what you can do.* "This is the time to show what you can do."

Bingo!

"Your final exams start in a couple of months, so I thought it would be a great experience to do another practice question and I can assess how you do." He looks at the class like he's offered us each a stash of money.

"A great experience?" I mutter. Highlighter Girl turns her head away from me. Taking this test will be as great as smashing my head through that window.

I can't do this.

It's okay for the Elliots in the room. He'll storm this assessment whereas I'll sit here struggling to spell *storm*. It was only yesterday when the teacher was laughing at me in Maths because I was writing about acute angels instead of angles.

"When I say so, I would like you to turn over the paper and read the short story on the other side. Then you have three ten-mark questions to answer, all assessing a variety of ..." Marshall's annoying voice fades into the distance. Despite my *improved* effort this year, the teachers are very clear that my grades are still *disappointing* and *unsatisfactory*. If I want to get a place on the joinery course at Farnham College, I must pass both Maths and English, but it's not that simple. I never finish tasks in time; I never remember anything and it's quite clear I can't spell. Mr Gregson, my science teacher, has told me, repeatedly, that if my handwriting doesn't improve, I'll need to use a laptop in lessons. I'll be one of the *special* kids. I don't blame him, even I struggle to read what I've written sometimes.

"Everyone ready?" Oh God, he's still talking and I'm still sitting here in this room, a head through the window seems the better option right now. "You've forty-five minutes starting from ... now!" He puts a large digital timer on the board and Highlighter Girl excitedly starts reading the paper, before long there's a rainbow of colours across her sheet. I look around the room and everyone's reading, except Lewis who's been moved to the back of the class for his *unacceptable behaviour* and looks like he's falling asleep.

Focus.

Read the first few lines.

Read them again.

Focus.

I keep forgetting what I've read.

Read it again.

Elliot's writing feverishly on the paper, not even coming up for a breath. The big timer's going down. Five minutes have passed. I read each word and try to get my head round this stupid story. It seems to be about a Snowdrop. A whole story about a Snowdrop! Why do I need to know about a Snowdrop if I want to cut up wood for a living? I look at the Macbeth display on the wall.

And for once, I understand what Shakespeare's getting at. I wish my scorpions would keep still and concentrate.

"Twenty minutes gone," Marshall informs us.

I don't need his reminder with that big timer mocking me. I've not even started a question yet. This is a joke. What's the point? I clench my fist and hit the table; Highlighter Girl shuffles her chair away from me. Marshall's beady eyes peer over the tower of exercise books he's marking; he gets up off his chair, striding over to my desk. "All okay, Josh?" I ignore him, bite hard on my lip, and try not to tell him where to shove this stupid story and his stupid lessons and his stupid moustache and his stupid wagging finger. Elliot stops writing for a second and looks over, mouthing something annoyingly encouraging at me. Sir points to the question paper. "What is it you are finding difficult?"

Where do I start, Sir?

I find it difficult that everyone else is halfway through writing their answers and I'm not even halfway through reading the first paragraph. I find it difficult that I'll always be the stupid one in the class. I find it difficult that no matter how hard I try—it doesn't seem worth it and, finally, I find it difficult that you're standing there and drawing more attention to me.

Anything else?

I find it difficult not to tell you what I really think about your lessons and your surprise tests. There's an awkward moment as he continues to stay by my table like a bad smell. Highlighter Girl glances over at me.

What's he waiting for?

Is he hoping that his mere god-like presence will suddenly make me become a genius?

Sadly not, Sir.

"Want some help, Josh?" Lewis has woken up and is shouting from the back of the room, mimicking Marshall's voice. "Your younger sister might be able to help you!" I spin round and there's a grin across his face. The chair crashes behind me as I jump up. The rest of the class freeze, some glance up from their papers hoping to see something more exciting than a story about Snowdrops. Marshall stands in my way and places a hand gently on my chest as Lewis' laughter bounces around the classroom walls. "Ha!" he shouts. "Did I hit a nerve?"

"Sit down, Josh. Leave it," Sir orders and then points at Lewis. "That's a second warning, Lewis. Keep up like that and—"

"Warning?" Lewis stands up whilst others put their pens down to watch the show. "How's that even fair? I'm not the one throwing chairs around the room! I was being kind and simply offering a suggestion. We all know Josh struggles at reading. I think you've set the bar too high, maybe he should start on Spot The Dog? I can get a copy from my—"

"What did you say?" I push past Marshall. "Say it again! Come on! I dare you to say it again!"

"Ignore him." Sir appears in front of me again. "I'll deal with him; you sit down and show me what you can do."

Everyone's staring. Elliot stands up and gently shakes his head at me as if to say *don't retaliate*. I look to Lewis, to Elliot and back to Marshall. "There's one thing I can do really, really well, Sir."

"What's that?"

I grab my bag and leave the classroom, shoving my shoulder into Lewis on the way out.

———

I hang around the park before it's time to collect Coral. She's waiting by the school gates of her primary school, swinging her blue school bag. She spots me and tilts her head, the same way Mum and the teachers tilt their heads, the what-have-you-done now head tilt. "I know! I know!" I raise my arms. "I'm only a few minutes late." She skips by my side.

"Tut, tut, tut." She waves her finger. "Mummy will be cross."

"Well, let's not tell her. Enough about me. How was your day, shrimp?"

Since Mum's been working more hours in the shop and Coral, my younger sister, has started school, I've been tasked with the job of collecting her two days a week. "It was good and bad. Good because we had jacket potatoes with beans and cheese for lunch but bad because Miss Sweeney made us do a test."

We turn left onto a narrow street and head towards our new home. Coral grabs my hand. We moved into a smaller terraced house a few months after our alcoholic stepdad Steve left and after I found out that Gavin Turner, my bio-dad, was in prison for assaulting two women. "How'd the test go?"

"Booooring!" she shouts. I smile and she squeezes my hand tightly. "How was your day, Joshy?"

"Actually, I had a test too."

"Was it difficult? Mine was very difficult. I had to spell words with the *oo* sound."

"Yes, mine was very difficult too."

"Well, you can only do your best, Joshy. That's what Miss Sweeney says. You can only do your best." She nods her head with each word.

We reach our house and walk up the cobbled path whilst I root for the house key in my trouser pocket. Mum's voice can be heard from behind the front door, she must've left work early. I open the door and hear my name. "I'm worried about him, Vee." She's on the phone to Elliot's mum. "School phoned again today. He shouted at another boy and stormed out of class." I look at Coral and raise my finger to my lips. "I know, Vee. I do. But what if?" I lean closer to the door. "What if ... he can have such a temper on him at times and I'm worried." Coral starts to fuss but I put my hand over her mouth. "What if? I hate saying this out loud and I would never say it to him but ..." Coral squirms and tries to pry my hand from her mouth. "What if ... it's how he learned to be? What if it's not his fault? I know. I know. I'm being silly, but what if he turns out like *him*? What if he turns out like Steve?"

My hand falls from Coral's face.

CHAPTER TWO

ELLIOT

Big, bright sunflowers bloom around her neck today. The thermometer in Mrs Spencer's office states twenty-six degrees. A warm March day for Mallowbank, one which promises Summer's waiting around the corner, or as Dickens would say 'when the sun shines hot, and the wind blows cold, when it is summer in the light and winter in the shade'. A day where school jumpers are tied around waists, shirt sleeves are rolled up, and water fights break out on the large fields behind the portacabins and yet, my school counsellor's wrapped up in one of her many colourful scarves. Sunflowers today, watermelons last week, and parrots the week before that.

Mrs Spencer takes a seat opposite me for our final meeting, hugging my red folder tight to her chest like a beloved childhood teddy. "I can't believe this day has finally come," she stutters, reaching for the box of tissues, dabbing her eyes and smearing black mascara across her cheek. Mrs Spencer and I have been meeting for two years now. Once a week, I have sat in this cluttered room, amongst the tattered self-help books and discarded art projects, vomiting up personal baggage whilst Mrs Spencer has kindly offered me advice, a smile, and a variety of questionable confectionery. Whilst I coughed up each ugly Elliot Hart furball, she's listened and comforted me: agoraphobic Mum furball, bully Josh furball, and not forgetting the evil Gavin Turner furball; Mrs Spencer's always been there with wise words and soft chocolate digestives.

"Elliot, Elliot, Elliot." She swings her lime green stockinged legs back and forth. "Lost in that world of yours again? This is it! Our last session. I look at the young man sitting in front of me—" She sniffs, pressing the tissue towards her mouth and starts to squeak, the next few words are barely audible but along the lines of *You've been through so much, I'm so proud of you* and finally, *I'm really going to miss you*. Each word spat out before taking a much-needed breath. It's March and our study leave doesn't start till June so, technically speaking, she would still see me around school, but this doesn't feel like a moment to be Elliot the Pedantic. I'll miss her too; her bright coloured clothes; how her feet never touch the ground and how she always offers me confectionery a month past their sell by date. I lean forward and pick up my rucksack, unzip it and search past my Tupperware box and tattered copy of Huxley's *Brave New World*, before pulling out a small parcel wrapped in yesterday's newspaper. My cheeks suddenly feel very warm. "I got you a little something Miss—it's nothing big and I'm sorry about the wrapping but well—well—I wanted to say ..."

Mrs Spencer has helped, *not* cured, my social anxiety.

She gently places my folder down on a plastic chair beside her and smiles. "Still one with the words?"

"I want to say thank you." The words spill out quickly, my arm outstretched, holding the parcel like an awkward child offering a gift at Christmas.

She takes it, presses it towards her chest and scrunches up her face. "It should be me thanking *you*, Elliot. You've taught me so much. You've taught me how to face life's challenges with such strength and dignity." My body tenses, as she gently tears off the newspaper wrapping, and I wish I opted for a box of Celebrations from Mr Peter's shop instead. Looking out of the window, there's a group of girls from the year below playing hockey in their PE lesson. "Oh! Elliot! I love it!" With one flick of her hand, a cotton scarf with all the colours of the rainbow emblazoned on it, floats in the air and falls delicately onto her knee. "It's absolutely beautiful. Thank you."

We remain silent.

Miss looks at her new scarf whilst I spot some students truanting their lesson, heading across the school yard towards the oak tree for a cigarette. She senses my uneasiness and comes to sit near me, holding her present in one hand and grabbing my hand tightly in the other. "Please listen to me. You're going to be okay. You're not the same frightened boy I came across two years ago. Since then, you've tackled many demons in your closet with such stoicism. Granted, you still need to work on your social skills." She winks. "But you've come through the worst and now it's your time to shine. Your mum's getting better every day—"

And there she had it.

Smack.

Bang.

Wallop.

Hitting the nail on the ginger Elliot Hart head.

"What is it? You've that puckered up face I've come to know *and* love so well. Is it Josh? He's not bullying you again?"

"Oh no! We're good. He's been different since our trip away."

"Is it your mum? She's getting better, isn't she? The last report from social services said—"

"Yeah, she is." I interrupt. "Honestly, she's much better. She's keeping up with her medication and her appointments with Dr. Jonas, walking to the village by herself and has even started an art course at the library, made friends with some guy called Clint." His name sounds sour in my mouth.

Mrs Spencer throws her arms in the air. "That sounds great!"

It is ... *great*. It's something I have wished for since I was small. My mum *is* getting better every day. Then why did it leave a big, tangly knot in my stomach?

"Doesn't it sound great, Elliot?" Miss questions.

"Yes, but–but ..."

"But-but what?"

I wrap the strap of my rucksack tight around my index finger. "It's silly. I guess I feel a bit weird. The one thing I knew about my life, the one thing that never changed, was my relationship with my mum. She was unwell, and I was her carer. That was fixed. The constant. I did the shopping, bills, cleaning; I went to the village and picked our food for that night. Everyone keeps talking about life after our exams, college or jobs, and I've spent so long thinking about my mum that I've no idea what I should do with my *own* life now!" My shoulders slump, weighed down by the honesty of these worries.

Mrs Spencer lets go of my hand and leans back in her chair. "This is all perfectly understandable. There's a lot of change coming up. Let's focus on that, shall we? Have you had any more thoughts on your plans for next year? We've discussed applying for the college in Farnham. You're bright enough to study any subject you want, or ..." She jumps out of her chair. "Before I forget! Mr Kay popped by yesterday and wanted me to give you this." She roots through a pile on her desk and hands me a shiny brochure, an application form for a drama course at Cruxby Royal College of Arts. "He's always said how great you are in drama; he said your acting's good but your singing's incredible! Best he's ever heard he said. There's a fantastic drama course in the city, which is focused around acting and singing, you can even start at sixteen. He says it's one of the most esteemed drama courses in the country." She flicks her hand in the air and takes a bow. "You could be the next Laurence Olivier."

I place my bag down and open the brochure. "A vibrant community of musicians, actors and production artists in the heart of the city of Cruxby—"

"See!" Mrs Spencer flaps, her stockinged legs swinging faster. "How good does that sound? You might become famous, and I'll get invited onto a TV show to talk about Elliot Hart: The Early Years!"

I smile at her enthusiasm and continue reading. "We are committed to the development of each student's unique and individual practice—"

"You can stay there during the week too!" she interrupts, pointing at the brochure. "Look at Anchor Court, the accommodation, it sounds very swish. En-suite bathrooms!"

"And leave my mum?"

"Only if she's well enough. One step at a time. Have a read for now." She nods to the brochure.

Skimming through the pages, it explains the different modules, from contemporary theatre to building the ensemble, on the back page is a table breaking down the costs of each academic year. "Miss! It says the fees start at six thousand pounds! Six thousand pounds! They *start* at six thousand pounds. There's no way I can afford this." My heart sinks. We can barely manage to afford food at the end of the month. There're only so many meals you can make with cheap mincemeat from the local Co-op.

"I know! But Mr Kay explained to me that they offer two scholarships a year for exceptional students. You fit this category, Elliot. We can invite the tutors into school to see you perform and, alongside our references, they might offer you that scholarship and pay for it all. The course *and* the accommodation. Imagine that!" I stuff the application form in my bag. "Look, it's just a thought. You, out of anyone, deserves a break. Promise me you will think about it and discuss it with your mum? Now she's getting better, I think you should start thinking about what *you* want for *your* life."

"I'll think about it." She leans back, folds her arms, and raises an eyebrow. "I promise!" I've seen pictures of Cruxby Royal College of Arts on flyers in Mr Kay's room and thought it looked like Hogwarts! But I've never dared to dream about any kind of life after St. Cuthberts. I've spent the past two years simply dreaming my mum would be alive when I came home from school. I've sung a few times in our drama lessons, even persuaded my neighbour, Tom, to teach me how to play the guitar and not forgetting my outstanding performance as orphan number five in last year's Oliver production, but to get on this course I would need to perform solo in front of an audience ... no matter what Mr Kay believes, I'm not ready for stardom or scholarships.

Mrs Spencer squeezes my hand again. "You'll figure it out, I'm sure. Look, the bell's going to go for period three, and I've a little something for you too." She flaps around her office, rummaging through the pile of folders on her desk, all of which hold the fears and secrets of another St. Cuthbert's pupil. "Ahh! Here it is." She spins around, a huge smile across her face, holding a brand-new tan leather briefcase like it's a precious artefact from a museum. "You've had that tatty old school bag since I met you. Don't think I didn't notice that the zip doesn't work and the T-rex on the front needs to remain in the Jurassic period." I want to correct her to the late Cretaceous period but realise, again, this is *not* the time.

See! My social skills are improving!

Handing over the briefcase, I resist the urge to tell her this might attract the attention I've been trying so hard to avoid and Tom gave me this *tatty old school bag* for Christmas. It was around the time Mum stopped leaving the house. You can just about make out T-Rex's open mouth and the faded blue words *You're Roar-Some* etched above. The school bell rings. We both stand and I'm not sure what the etiquette is to say goodbye to your school counsellor, so I stretch my arm out to shake her hand but suddenly find myself smothered in her chest and surrounded by sunflowers. "You're one of life's good ones, Elliot Hart," she whispers into my ear. "Don't be scared to dream."

CHAPTER THREE

JOSH

Mum wipes the kitchen counter and then twists her hair up the back of her head, fastening it with a clip, whilst I varnish a small piece of wood at the table.

"How was school yesterday?"

Finally, she wants to talk to me and not Elliot's mum! Last night, we had tea together and watched Eastenders, but she didn't mention the phone call from Marshall and I certainly didn't bring up the conversation I overheard. How can she think that I could be anything like that monster? But if I'm honest, I worry about the father figures in my life. My bio-dad's in prison for assaulting women and my step-dad's a violent drunk. What hope do I have?

"It was fine." There's a part of me that wants to tell her that I'm struggling in lessons, but I don't want to see that look of disappointment again. I *do* want to tell her I've had enough. I want to tell her that if one more teacher tells me to *spell it out* when I get a word wrong, that I might grab their green pen and shove it up their nose. Why does it matter anyway? If you can understand what I've written, how about *not* correcting it and then we can both leave the lesson happy. I want to tell her that no matter how many spelling tests they give me, I still won't get it correct, and if I do get it right one week, there's absolutely no guarantee I will get it right the week after. Pure fluke! Roll with it! I slap another layer of varnish on the wood and remain mute instead.

Since we moved into this smaller house, I've been trying to help Mum as much as I can, even making some furniture with my mediocre woodwork skills, some shelves for the girls' room, and a table for the living room, seeing the designs in my mind is much easier than understanding the stories in English or the boring articles in history. Mr Hogg lent me a couple of saws; a chisel and mallet and I've created a little workshop in the shed at the bottom of the garden.

"They've asked me to do an extra shift at the shop this evening," Mum shouts over the noise of CBeebies on the television. "The girls have been fed but Coral still needs to do her phonics homework." Mum's been working at the gift shop in Mallowbank since Steve left. Recently, they've given her a set of keys and put her in charge of closing. We moved into this house near the dogs' home last year, and even though I go to sleep listening to the chorus of barking, I like it. Mum let me have the tiny third bedroom and the girls share the larger one. I don't mind that it's the size of a toilet cubicle. It's my own space. My early teenage years were spent sharing with Coral and her hoard of broken dolls and Peppa Pig toys. I'm grateful to wake up without Barbie's left foot sticking up my nose. The day we moved into this house, me and Mum shared a Chinese takeaway and made a promise to each other. I promised to *stay* out of trouble, and she promised to avoid men that *are* trouble. So far, she seems to be keeping to her word, and apart from slight hiccups like in English, I'm *trying* to keep to my promise too ... even if she doesn't see it.

Luckily, there's been no sight of Steve since he walked out that Christmas, so I wonder if he's moved out of Mallowbank altogether and Mum's doing much better, even talking about going to college to study business management. The girls haven't asked much about him either, probably happy to see the back of his drunk arse. Mum wipes a mark off her black skirt and looks at her watch before kneeling by Coral, who's colouring in a picture of Skye from Paw Patrol. "Okay, I'm off sweetheart. Josh is going to help with your phonics tonight." She leans down and gently plants a kiss on her forehead, before tickling Sapphire's belly, who's starfished on the settee, hypnotised by the cartoons on the television. After repeating my instructions for the evening once more, she leaves for work and locks the door behind her. A habit she picked up since Steve left.

"Right, squirt." I close the colouring book. "Let's do this homework and then have some chocolate chip ice cream I spotted in the freezer." Her dog-eared blue exercise book is on the kitchen table underneath some post. There's a thin, brown envelope with a red St. Cuthbert's stamp in the corner. What do *they* want? One bust up in English and they are writing home already. I used to fall out with Marshall every soddin' week. I rip it open and scan through the letter. It's the progress report they send out in the last term and they're inviting Mum into school to *discuss my progress*. They've kindly included a sheet of paper with a colourful table on it, my subjects all coloured green, orange or red. Green means all is great in the world, orange means we're worried and red means you're going to spend your older years working in the fast-food restaurant outside of Mallowbank. The amount of red on my sheet of paper indicates that I'm *underachieving* in all subjects except design and technology and PE. I bet Marshall would love to discuss the symbolism of these colours.

Red.

The colour of anger. Red suggests my teachers are livid

about my *lack of progress*. The letter finishes with their concern about me passing my end of year exams. Great.

"Joshy," Coral tugs at my school trousers and waves her reading book in her hand. "Miss Sweeney says I've to read this book with a grown up and answer the questions at the back, something about Buff and Klipper."

I place the letter back down on the kitchen table and take a seat, allowing Coral to jump onto my knee and rest her head on my shoulder. "Okay, squirt." I flip the book over and start reading the back, Coral starts laughing. "What's up with you, giggler?"

"You! You're so funny!"

I tickle her sides and she squirms on my knee, laughing even harder. "Now, come on! Focus. We haven't even started the story yet!" I continue reading and she squeals louder, so I place the book down. "What's up now?"

"You've already said that line, silly!" I start again but she turns and pants at me, her cheeks red from laughter. "You sound strange when you read." She mimics my voice whilst moving her arms like a robot.

"You know what?" I shove her off my knee. "Leave it."

"No! Mummy said—"

"I don't care what Mummy said." She runs off to the living room. I wonder what other sixteen-year-old boys are doing this evening and I doubt many are reading about the adventures of Biff and sodding Kipper whilst being mocked by their little sister. I storm out of the kitchen, slamming the door behind me and head down the narrow garden path to the rickety shed at the end. It's a tiny space but I've managed to makeshift a bench and nailed the tools that Mr Hogg gave me onto the wall. I'm making Mum something, the joints are small and fiddly, so I choose a fret saw but make a mistake and the wood splinters. There's a photo stuck to the back of the shed door. It's of the Christmas I spent at Elliot's house when we came back from Cruxby, all squished into his kitchen, our mums, my sisters, and Tom. I think back to that Josh who thought he *could* change.

I was wrong.

I'm predictable Josh.

I'm disappointment Josh.

I'm a cause for concern Josh.

I'm *turn out like Steve* Josh.

CHAPTER FOUR

ELLIOT

The school bell rings to signal the end of the day as I leave the science classroom, snaking through the crowded corridor. Felicity Hooper runs to catch up with me. "Hi!"

I turn to face her, struggling to hide the daft smile which involuntarily appears when she's around. "Hi."

"New bag?"

I look at the briefcase in my hand and my toes curl. "This? Yeah. A present from Mrs Spencer yesterday. Maybe she's testing my resilience to bullies?"

She laughs. "Don't be silly. That's really sweet of her. There're not many people who can pull off a bag like that, but you sure can." I'm not sure if that's a compliment. "I saw you coming out of her office. Everything okay?" Over the last year, I've firmly set up camp in the friend zone with Felicity Hooper. *Damn it.* I haven't simply set up a camp. I've pitched a tent, set a fire, and started cooking some sausages in this camp! We chat in lessons about work, occasional messages about homework deadlines and books, but I'll soon be the boy she's going to talk to about other boys.

"I'm fine." I offer to take the pile of textbooks she's

carrying. "It was my last session with her. It appears I'm all fixed!"

"That's wonderful!" She wraps her arms around me, and I use all my strength to stand upright and not become a messy schoolboy heap on the polished floor. When she pulls away, I notice the recent sunny weather has multiplied the freckles across her nose. "You're doing so well. I'm very proud of you. Now, come here." She grabs my hand and drags me to the drama noticeboard. "I want to know what your thoughts are on this." Photos from last year's Oliver production are still pinned up. Felicity looks amazing, centre stage, as Nancy in a long navy-blue skirt and floaty white blouse. She points to a notice:

ST. CUTHBERT'S
TALENT SHOW

AUDITIONS:
MONDAY 21ST MARCH
(LUNCHTIME)
IN THE DRAMA STUDIO

EVERYONE
WELCOME!

She looks at me with her big, brown eyes. "It's next Monday. I've put my name down already, decided this is my opportunity to show my parents that I'm destined to study drama next year, and have already rehearsed an Alan Bennett monologue. Want to hear it?" I nod and she stands back, lifts her head in the air, her expression now solemn and poised. "The policeman said did I want to see where it happened? I said what good will that do?" She breaks into a smile. "Did you like it? It's about a grieving wife discussing her husband who died when his motorbike crashed."

"Light-hearted then?" I laugh.

She giggles. "Yeah, it's pretty intense stuff but hopefully I can pull it off."

"Course you will! Mr Kay loves you and you're incredibly talented. I still dream about you as Nancy. Not dream! Remember! I still *remember* how good you were as Nancy. I didn't dream about you. Not that I wouldn't dream about you—"

"Thanks, Elliot." My cheeks grow hotter. "I'll never be as good a singer as you are though. I hear you in drama, even if you do hide away at the back. Anyway, I've been thinking, and I think you should put yourself forward. Mr Kay's always rambling on to the class about how great you are even if you *still* don't believe it."

I shake my head. "Sorry to disappoint you—"

"Really? We're back here again. After all you've been through!" She grabs my shoulders and looks me straight in the eyes and if I had the smallest bit of confidence, I would kiss her right here, right now, but instead I look to the floor. "People still talk about your infamous history speech, and I might be mistaken but The New York Times wrote a full article on your incredible portrayal of orphan number five." She laughs. "This is your final chance. It's the end of the road for us at St. Cuthbert's. Please. For me?" I think of the application form Mrs Spencer gave me yesterday which is still sitting in my bag. Singing is the only time I feel truly ... free, but the thought of performing solo in front of an actual audience and not just hidden away in a drama class or in the shower at home, makes me want to curl up in a ball and hide for eternity. "Elliot?"

"Yes?"

"Please say yes." Her big, brown eyes predictably work their magic.

"Okay," I mumble.

"What was that?" she squeals and lifts her arms in the air. "Say it louder, Bieber! Say it so everyone at St. Cuthbert's can hear. Was that a ... yes?" I quickly scribble my name on the paper and Felicity jumps up and down before hugging me tightly. We walk down the corridor, side by side, our hands so close that I can't help obsessing over what it would be like to wrap my fingers around hers.

"I don't suppose you've seen Josh lately?" I ask.

She shakes her head. "No. I wouldn't want to, either. I know you've forgiven him for the bullying, but I can't. Why?"

"He had a bust up with Lewis in English on Tuesday."

She throws her arms in the air. "Quelle surprise!"

"Lewis was teasing him about his reading. I think he's really struggling, and he's changed from the boy who bullied me. Honestly!"

She links my arm with hers. "We'll have to agree to disagree on that one. Anyway, enough about Josh McBride. I still can't believe we'll be leaving this place in a few months. Have you decided what you're doing next year? Did Mr Kay mention the drama course in Cruxby to you too?"

"Yeah. Mrs Spencer showed me the brochure."

"Have you given it any thought? I had a look, and it sounds amazing. I think I'm going to apply but I need to convince my parents that acting's for me and crush *their* lifelong dreams of me being a doctor." She rolls her eyes. "I don't think this news will go down very well with my dad but if I tell him about some of the famous actors that attended Cruxby Royal—"

"I won't be going."

She stops and looks at me. "Oh no! Why?"

How should I put this in a way someone like Felicity will understand? Because I don't have six thousand pounds hiding away in my piggybank and I don't live in a big mansion on the other side of Mallowbank with my two rich parents. I live in a small, pokey, terraced house with one unemployed parent who's *doing their best*. I'm offered free meals at school and budget our benefits each month to make sure we've enough money to eat.

"It's not really for me. I'm going to go to Farnham college and do Maths or something."

Her face falls. "And there's me thinking we could apply for the same course but not to worry, I'm sure you can do anything with that big brain of yours." She taps my head and looks upward. "I would sell my actual soul to go to Cruxby Royal College of Arts."

"If you did, would you lend me the money?" I grin.

She smiles back. "But my dad won't let it happen. Get a good job, Felicity he says." She wiggles her finger to impersonate her father. "Get a good job that gives you security, that's what's important in this life. How romantic does that sound, Elliot? Security? Let the word roll off your tongue. Se-cur-ity."

I open the school doors for her, and we make our way out of the building and into the bright sunshine, swallowed by the tide of students heading home for the day. "That doesn't seem fair. You should be able to do what you want to do. Oh! Before I forget. Where are you up to with *Brave New World*?" Since last year, we've had this thing where we read the same book at the same time. It's like our own mini book club. So far this year, we've discovered the wonder of *The Book Thief*, *Animal Farm* and *The Road*. Now, we're on Huxley's masterpiece.

She grabs my arm. "Well ... I stayed up late last night and finished chapter fifteen." Breaking away from the large crowds, we walk across the field discussing the drama of chapter fifteen and how scary Huxley's futuristic society is. Felicity looks up to the cloudless sky and breathes in. "I want to read *Fahrenheit 451* next. I've heard it's as good as *Brave New World*. My dad said he would get it for me for my next birthday." She looks across the field. "Don't you love this time of year, Elliot? Honestly, once I see the daffodils sprouting it feels like a new start, and anything's possible. Don't you think so?" I wish I had some of her optimism for the future, but I do feel such positivity is easier when Daddy has a rich job and a spare six thousand pounds in his account. "Anyway, I need to head off. Violin lessons tonight." She rolls her eyes again before skipping off in the opposite direction to my house.

I wander home through the narrow-terraced streets to the poorer side of Mallowbank. It's still warm and mums have brought their wooden kitchen chairs out to the front garden to catch the evening sun, little children ride their bikes down the road, and some have even managed to persuade their parents to get the paddling pools out. There's a smell of barbeques drifting in the air and an ice-cream van sings its cheerful tune in the distance. I walk easier nowadays. The heavy weight of worrying what I would find behind my front door has lightened since our trip to Cruxby. Mum's still at the end of all my thoughts, but the feeling's not as intense, not as consuming. The ghost that would follow me each day, prodding me in the back and questioning, how's your mum today? Is she out of bed? Is she alive? That ghost is quieter now. As I turn onto Ivygreen Road, I lift my head to the sky and feel the sun on my face.

Once through my front door, I find Mum in the corner of our living room, which she turned into her little art studio a few months ago. A row of paint pots stand on the windowsill and her easel is propped in the corner with her latest creation resting on it. Mum insisted this section of the house caught the best light and what did it matter if we could only see one half of the television screen. She turns, paintbrush in one hand and another nestling in her red curly hair. Her apron's covered with an explosion of colour.

We smile.

Words aren't needed anymore. We used to feel the need to explicitly state whether her day had been *good* or *bad*, but we don't do this now. A luxury I don't take for granted either. We appreciate the little things. Mum says I can find a silver lining in everything, but I must salvage some good from the past few years, otherwise, what's the point? We don't really talk about Gavin Turner and what he did to her. I don't want to. He can rot in jail for all I care. I do understand Mum must come to terms with her past, but I hope Dr. Jonas is unravelling that mess with her.

She looks at the briefcase. "New bag?"

"Yeah. Mrs Spencer gave it to me. It was our last appointment yesterday."

Mum smiles. "That's good. How did it go? What did you talk about?"

I decided not to tell her about the drama course, unless we find six thousand pounds down the back of the sofa or I develop a super power to perform on stage, neither look likely to happen anytime soon. "Nothing important."

"What do you think of this?" She nods to her latest piece on the easel, a secluded cottage in a woodland covered in snow, tyre tracks head off into the distance and lots of little footprints lead to the front door.

I place my bags down on the carpet. "It's amazing as per usual. Who's it for?"

"A lovely lady in Farnham. She sent a photograph of where she used to spend her family holidays when she was young.

Her and seven brothers! Imagine that! They would stay in this cottage every Christmas. Imagine the memories they created inside this very building, eight little stockings hanging above the fireplace." We lose ourselves in someone else's past. A dangerous habit of ours. Putting my arm around her, she rests her head on my chest. Over the past two years I've grown much taller which only seems to accentuate my ungainliness and awkwardness. I'm now a really long matchstick. We stare at the painting, and I'm astonished by her talent, even noticing how she's used blue paint for the snow to make it realistic.

"How did you sell it?"

"Clint helped me," she replies. "He advertised some of my work on his website and people got in touch. Four commissions so far!" Her voice is childlike, proudly telling me of her latest achievements. I pull away and she places her paintbrush back in the jar. "What is it?"

"Nothing." Sitting on the settee, I take off my school shoes and switch the television on so I can watch half of the evening news. Mum puts her hands on her hips and stands in the way.

"What is it?" She presses on. "Dr. Jonas says we must communicate our feelings. Why's your face like that?"

I peer around her. "It's not like anything."

"Yes, it is! It's all scrunched up. Is it my painting? Is it Josh? Is it Clint?" I'm annoyed at myself for feeling this way whenever she mentions his name, which has been *a lot* over the last couple of months. Clint loves her art. Clint thinks she has potential. Clint is wonderful. Good, old Clint. It's a wonder we ever survived without Clint in our lives. Mum unties her apron and hangs it over the easel, sitting down beside me whilst I carry on pretending to watch the news. "It's been well over a year now since I was admitted to hospital, and I'm doing much better. We both know that. You need to stop worrying. I've attended every single counsellor session, kept up with my medication. Clint's a nice man, a friend, who attends the art classes with me at the library. That's all."

I rest my head on her shoulder. How do I tell her? I'm not sulking like a petulant toddler because I'm worrying about *her*. It's because I'm worrying about *myself*. That's it. I'm going to hell. I should be shouting from the rooftops of Mallowbank, holding a huge banner, and waving a foam finger, my mum gets up, dresses, leaves the house, paints, and is making new friends. How wonderful is that? Yet here I am sulking like a six-year-old jealous of the new boy in class. Poor Elliot, my mum doesn't need me anymore. Poor Elliot wants to go to drama college but doesn't want an audience. Poor Elliot's poor and can't afford the damn college anyway! I grab my copy of *Brave New World* from my bag and the college application falls out onto the floor.

"What's this?" Mum goes to reach for it, but I manage to snatch it first and stuff it back in my bag.

"Nothing." I stutter. "It's about a trip coming up with school."

She ruffles my hair and goes back to her painting. "A school trip? Do we need to pay for it? Money's tight again this month."

CHAPTER FIVE

JOSH

It's Friday and Marshall's arranged a meeting with Mum and Mrs Stephens to discuss my progress, or *lack of*, at school. Personally, I can think of numerous better ways to spend my afternoon than having a cosy chat with Mum and Marshall. The small, silver lining in this whole sorry scenario is I don't have to be in science with Mr Gregson. Coral's at school but Mum couldn't find a babysitter, so this toe-curling meeting will also be attended by Saff, who currently has melted chocolate buttons plastered to both cheeks. "Here, hold her." Mum passes me the chocolate monster, whilst getting a hand mirror out of her bag and reapplying her red lipstick.

"What the hell are you doing?"

"What?" She feigns innocence, pulling out a tissue and pressing her lips down on it. "Simply trying to make a good impression, that's all." She reaches for Saff. "This school has given you a lot of chances, and I'm not sure how many more you have left. I need to make a good impression. It's in *your* best interests."

"*My* best interests?"

"Yes. *Yours.*" She smiles, showing some lipstick on her front tooth.

"Let me get this correct. You're making a good impression by making yourself look like a clown?"

"Josh!" Saff releases herself from Mum's grip and makes a run for it down the long corridor. In a couple of months this final year will be over, and I can get out of the St. Cuthbert hell-hole forever.

"A clown that's losing patience with you. I need to do whatever it takes, son." She blows me a kiss. "Whatever it takes."

Marshall opens his office door and gestures for us both to come in. "Good afternoon, Ms McBride. Josh."

Mum follows him into his office. "Mum!" I point down the corridor. "Saff? Your daughter? Or are we leaving a two-year-old to explore the school by herself?"

"Can you get her Joshy sweetheart?" *Joshy sweetheart?* No! She didn't. Did she? Did Mum give Marshall the eye? As of tomorrow, I'm putting myself up for adoption. After grabbing my little sister before she joins a year seven class studying A Midsummer Night's Dream, me and Mum take a seat in Marshall's small office. The walls are lined with shelves of old books and there's a small window looking out onto the two large tennis courts below. The noticeboard above his desk is full of photos, mostly of him and a woman who I imagine is his wife, and two teenage girls. I forget teachers have lives and families outside of this prison. There's a younger Marshall in one of the photos, with a bald top lip, wearing a black hat and gown and standing with a man who must be his dad. A collection of mugs on his desk, one growing something Mr Gregson would happily use in his lessons. Mrs Stephens, my form tutor, bustles in, eating a sandwich and apologising for her lateness. She takes a seat behind the desk, next to Marshall, and introduces herself to Mum before explaining the reason for this torture. "We are all here this afternoon to discuss Josh and his progress in year eleven. You would've noticed from his last report that he's not hitting his target grades in nearly all his GCSE subjects." I stare at Marshall, wondering why he's even at this meeting, probably ordered in popcorn to enjoy the show. Saff waddles over to Mrs Stephens and reaches for her sandwich.

"It's important to acknowledge," Marshall interrupts. "All of Josh's teachers have commented on a vast improvement in his behaviour and attitude this year." Fat lot of good that's doing. I'm still the thicko at the bottom of the class, still in the bottom set for Maths with Benjamin-picks-his-nose-and-stares-out-the-window-Rivers and Max-can't-control-his-anger-and-throws-chairs-across-the-room-Robinson.

If someone listened to me for one damn second, I could explain that I *do* get it. I *can* work it out. It takes me a little bit longer and I don't know why, maybe Gavin Turner gave me a dud brain gene and part of my brain doesn't work like others. Then why's Elliot so annoyingly clever? He doesn't have a dud brain gene; he's destined to go to all the top universities and probably discover the cure for cancer. We're like twins separated at birth, an experiment to see how each will turn out. Ha! Look at this twin, try all he might, he will always be stupid.

Throw him away!

Discard him!

He's good for nothing!

"Josh," Marshall's staring at me. "Did you hear me? I was explaining to your mum that I've spoken to Mrs Stephens because I think there's something else going on. I've thought about it for a while so I can only apologise to both of you that it's taken this long to get a meeting organised and especially with your final exams on the horizon." Ahh, finally, someone else believes in the dud brain gene too! "We would like you to take a test."

"A test?" He does love his tests. All three of them are staring at me now. Saff sits down on the floor and finishes the sandwich. Miss looks at me and smiles whilst Mum mouths *sorry*.

"Sorry. Not a test. That's the wrong choice of words. A dyslexia screening. They can help give an indication of dyslexia. They don't provide a formal diagnosis but can help outline your strengths and weaknesses. After that, if needed, we can look at a formal diagnosis. The screening would allow us to see if there's a reason why you struggle at times, then we can give you the support you need *and* deserve, especially in the lead up to the exams. Everyone should have an equal starting point, shouldn't they?" I think of Steve and Gavin. My starting point has never been ... *equal*.

I need to plan an escape route before they pin me down and test me for dud brain genes. "I don't need a test and I don't need extra support. What I do need is for everyone to get off my friggin' back. You said my behaviour's improved. I've kept my part of the deal, Mum. If the grades aren't improving, you might have to simply accept that your son's stupid and leave it there."

"Josh!" Mum puts a hand on my leg and makes big eyes at Marshall. "I'm so sorry for his outburst. It's the stress of the exams and the final year." And the stress of my mum flirting with my English teacher.

"No need for apologies Ms McBride, maybe discuss it at home and let us know what you think but the exams are coming up soon, so I wouldn't want to wait too long. The screening's a simple one, Nina, one of our colleagues in the learning support department, will find out more about Josh to see how best he can be supported in the classroom. Following that, we can look at getting a diagnostic assessment carried out by a certified dyslexia assessor, and then at least—"

"Maybe you need a *diagnostic assessment* on your hearing," I interrupt.

"Josh!" Mum puts a hand on my arm. "I'm sorry. Again, it's the stress. He's had a lot to deal with at home and—"

"What? Did you not listen to me? I don't need a stupid test!" I stand up and Saff stretches her arms out to be picked up. "It would be a waste of everyone's time. We don't need a test to prove that I'm too stupid to pass these exams. This little get together." I wave my arm in the air. "Has been lovely but the sooner we accept that I'm a lost cause, the better for everyone. You're right Mum. There's no hope for me." I march out, leaving them all in silence except for Saff who's calling out my name. My heart beats hard against my chest. I don't see the point in any of this. I'm never going to pass these exams and I won't get onto the joinery course. I'll be *Joshy dumb dumb pants* forever, forced to retake the year and sit in classes with the younger ones looking like Will Farrell in that Elf film the girls watch at Christmas. I look at my watch, still twenty minutes of period four left, but instead of turning right to join Mr Gregson talking about acids and alkalis, I walk out onto the yard and towards the old, oak tree.

The oak tree is where the smokers congregate at break and lunch, there's two rotten tree stumps that have become makeshift chairs and it's perfectly situated out of sight of the teachers. Although, I think they know about this place and it's easier to ignore. Freddie Rothwell, a boy who was forced to retake this year, is standing by the tree smoking. Freddie looks tough, like a villain in the cartoon films the girls watch, black hair, dark eyes, tall, looking like he should be attending nightclubs not high school. His skin's covered in pitted scars, and he's always scowling. A lot of rumours about Freddie float around St. Cuthbert's and Mallowbank: dad's in jail, he always carries a knife in his trouser pocket, and he once knocked somebody's two front teeth out because they called him Frederick. I see him with Lewis sometimes or standing in the corridor after being sent out of his lessons, even the teachers are scared of Freddie Rothwell. I turn to walk back to the school building.

"Oi," he calls. I stop, turn, stand a bit taller. His eyes narrow and I think he's deciding whether to start a fight or a conversation with me. He's working out if I'm worth his time. "You the boy who punched the ginger kid last year?"

My heart sinks, suppose some rumours around school are true. I nod. Another stretch of silence as he continues to stare at me before pulling out a cig packet from his pocket. "Want one?" I've not smoked since me and Lewis used to hang out, but I step forward and take one, Freddie flicks his lighter, cupping his hands around the flame as I take a deep drag. My head pounds instantly and it makes me feel sick. Avoiding Freddie's intense gaze, I look down, kick the mud with my shoes, the second drag doesn't feel as bad.

"Haven't seen you around much." Freddie's voice is deep and gravelly. He doesn't have the same accent as those born in Mallowbank. "You used to hang out with Lewis?" He spits on the ground.

I kick some more mud and make a hole in the ground. "Yeah. We're not as tight now."

"Shame. He's a good 'un. Does as he's told. I'll be in the park later, you should come. I see you around school. There's somethin' about you. I think you're better than the rest of them round 'ere." He finishes his cig and flicks it into the bushes. "I'll see you at the park. Nine o'clock. Don't be late."

CHAPTER SIX

ELLIOT

After pouring myself some orange juice, I grab a soft Rich Tea biscuit from the paper plate. I've been attending the Young Carers meetings on a Friday evening at Mallowbank Community Centre since my trip to Cruxby with Josh to find Gavin Turner. Mrs Spencer got in touch with some local schools and helped get the sessions started. It was surprising to realise there are other young carers in the area. A meeting was arranged with Mum and our social worker, and it was agreed Mum would attend her counselling sessions with Dr Jonas and I would attend these monthly meetings. They haven't been too insufferable. There's usually around four or five of us, sitting on uncomfortable plastic chairs with Glenn, the leader, sitting at the front.

Grabbing one of the chairs, I sit myself down and recognise three familiar faces this month. George, a tall boy who spends the meetings slouched in his chair hiding underneath his New York Yankees baseball cap. He attends the high school in Farnham and his dad left when he was young. His mum's recently been diagnosed with Motor Neurone disease, a rare condition that affects her brain and I don't think there's a cure. George only speaks when he's spoken to and often that's a simple grunt. Glenn doesn't push it; I think he's thankful he turns up each month. We often get carers that attend for one meeting and then vanish. Sitting next to George is Katie, a small elf-like girl with blond hair who I recognise from the year below at St. Cuthbert's. She's the polar opposite of George and loves to talk. Tom would say she has verbal diarrhoea. Her younger brother has cerebral palsy and has frequent appointments at the hospital. It sounds like he takes up a lot of her parents' time. To the right of me is Frankie, a hot-headed girl, who we've come to realise is dealing with *anger issues*. Her mum's a recovering addict and I think social services insisted she attended these meetings. She spends most of the time scowling at all of us and peeling the skin from around her fingernails. Cradling my plastic cup of orange juice, we all sit in comfortable silence whilst Glenn gets ready for the meeting.

"Good evening." Glenn always wears tight blue jeans, off-white Converse trainers and a woolly jumper, no matter how hot it is outside. He never stands up to welcome the group but sits, legs apart, leaning forward, to create the illusion we are simply at home discussing what to watch on the telly. He's saving up to go to university next year and he thought volunteering would look good on his application form but personally, I think he actually enjoys leading this group. He has endless patience with Frankie and always finds time to chat with George when we're doing an activity. His deep voice echoes around the room and the fluorescent lights start to give me a headache. I look at my watch, 7:10 pm. Only fifty minutes left. "How are we—"

"Sorry!" The door barges open and a girl storms through, takeaway coffee in one hand, she takes off her sunglasses and surveys the room. "Sorry I'm late. You know, trouble at home. Ha! You do know!" She laughs. We all stare, even George glances up briefly from under his cap. It's exciting to have a new face come and join our hapless group. "I'm in the right place, aren't I? Messed up families R us?"

Glenn stands up. "Ah!" He looks at the sheet on his clipboard. "Ruby Flanagan? I was hoping you would turn up." He strides over and offers a hand to shake. "Nice to meet you. I'm Glenn, the leader. Please take a seat and—"

"Glyn!" Her voice is loud and confident. "Nice to meet you, too. I take it it's your job to listen to all our crap, yeah? Well take a seat my friend and buckle in. I've a lot!" She marches over to the empty seat by me, smiles, winks and sits down leaving Glenn still standing, arm outstretched.

"Well," he mutters, returning to his chair. "I'm not here to listen to your ... *crap*. This is a safe space for you and, everyone else, to discuss your—"

"Yeah! Yeah!" Ruby waves her arm in the air and leans back in her chair. Her hair's short and London-bus-red and she's wearing a tartan shirt over a white vest top, baggy denim jeans and a pair of Doc Martens. "I get it, Glyn. My dad says I must come to these meetings if I want to be insured on his car when I turn seventeen, seems a crazy deal to me but whatever floats his boat, but ... woah. Biscuits!" She springs out of her chair and heads to the table in the corner, grabbing a handful of digestives and pouring herself some juice. Katie's sitting, mouth open wide, and George smirks. "Sorry." Crumbs spill out of her mouth. "I'm definitely shutting up now. First meeting nerves. My bad." She smiles and pretends to pull a zip across her mouth and presses her lips tight together. "Fire away, Glyn!" she mumbles.

"It's not ..." He shakes his head and Ruby falls back into her chair. "Never mind. Right, shall we start? I'll quickly run through how the meetings work for our newcomer. We go around the group, and if you wish, you share how things are at home. We chat, honestly and openly, without judgement and whatever we discuss does not leave this building. Unless I have cause for concern for your welfare."

"Like Fight Club?" Ruby leans in and whispers. "What stays in messed up lives R us, stays in messed up lives R us." I laugh and Glenn frowns at me.

"After our group discussion, we complete a fun activity."

"Spoiler." I shake my head and whisper to Ruby, "It's not fun."

George pulls his cap farther over his eyes and slouches down in his chair. "And then," Glenn continues. "We usually finish up discussing what we hope for in the future and how maybe we can make that happen." My thumb pierces through the plastic. I hate speaking in front of people. I'm more of a listener. Always have been. Introvert. It must be God's sick joke to make me love singing and performing *but* make me hate being watched. It doesn't matter how big or small, I hate *all* audiences. I've absolutely no control how red my face goes when I speak out loud, or how squeaky my damn voice is. How can I ever dream of applying for drama college if I can't speak in front of these five people? Katie starts sharing, chatting in length about school and a party that she's been invited to, when Glenn asks how her brother's doing, she cleverly avoids the question like a skilled politician and brings the topic back to herself. My hands feel sweatier, so I plan what I will say in my head first to see if it helps.

What do I want to say?

My mum's doing well, and I'm annoyed because, it turns out, I'm a selfish, egotistical brat. That should do it. Young carer's annoyed he doesn't have to care as much. We listen to Frankie briefly tell us what a waste of space her mum is, and George grunts and shrugs his shoulders.

Glenn tilts his head. "Elliot, would you like to share?"

"My mum's doing well." I splutter. "She's painting." My face is already hot. Ruby's staring at me. What magical powers would it take to get the community centre floor to open and suck me down into a deep, black hole? I remember seeing the news recently and there was a huge sinkhole in America, that's exactly what I need right now.

"That's good." Glenn praises. "And how do you feel about that?"

Confused. Guilty. Angry. Lonely. Jealous. "I feel fine, thank you." Glenn takes my tomato cheeks as a cue to move swiftly on.

"Ruby, usually on a first meeting, you give a little bit of information about yourself and why you're here, but only if you want to." It's sad that someone as confident as her is carrying her own invisible baggage too. These meetings leave me feeling angry and jealous of other sixteen year olds. We're teenagers. We only get to be teenagers once. We should be hanging out in the park, arguing with our parents about what time we must be home or lying carefree in our messy rooms listening to music.

We definitely shouldn't be here.

We have all our older years to be stressed about mortgages and jobs and children. We are young and should be carefree.

Carefree.

Free of care.

Free of worry.

Free.

I can't ever imagine what that would feel like. Even now, I still worry about Mum's depression, her wolf. I worry the wolf will prowl around our house and find her again. I worry there might be a day I come home from school and find her in her bed. Vacant. When a student at school complains that their parents won't buy them the latest phone, I think they should spend ten minutes with this group. Their problems might not seem as big then. All eyes, except George's, land on the girl with the bright red hair and dark lipstick. She pulls out her chewing gum and puts it in the empty plastic cup. "Sure, Glyn. My mum has terminal ovarian cancer. The nurses that visit the house don't think she has long left. By that, I mean she will die soon. No one ever seems to use the word die, do they?

Passed away.

Left us.

Laid to rest.

Deceased.

Didn't make it.

Didn't make what? I think we should say it how it is. My mum will die, and it will be soon." The room falls silent. George lifts his head and takes his cap off. "I also have three annoying younger brothers and a dad who's *doing his best*, working all the hours he can as a police officer in Cruxby and looking after my mum, me, and the boys. But he needs help. I can see that. So, I step up as much as I can, and I come here if he wants me to." She bites down on her bottom lip and stares at Glenn, raising one manicured eyebrow to say *I'm finished.*

"Do you get support at home then?" Glenn's voice is soft and sincere.

"Yeah. Some Macmillan nurses come round each day."

"That's good. Thanks for sharing, Ruby. I'm sorry about your mum's illness. That must be really difficult," he replies.

Ruby shrugs and puts another piece of chewing gum in her mouth. "It is what it is, Glyn. Can't change it." Noticing the mood in the room turn more sombre, Glenn swiftly introduces this month's *fun* activity, proudly bringing out some blank A4 paper and a margarine tub full of felt tips, most without a lid.

"We're going to choose a partner and draw their faces, keeping it positive please!" Glenn smiles. "Sometimes, we fail to see how others see us." Ah, the joyous task of choosing a partner strikes again, adults do like to humiliate us. The teachers specifically *love* it. Choose a partner! Enjoy that moment of sheer panic. What if no one chooses me? What if I'm left on my own? What lifelong trauma will this leave me with? Katie quickly claims George, the silent one being a smarter decision than the angry one. Glenn partners with Frankie, which leaves me with Ruby. She turns and smiles.

Having someone stare at me for so long and so close makes my cheeks flush. I hope Glenn has lots of red felt tips in that old margarine tub of his. My eyes remain fixed on my own masterpiece; it's apparent I haven't inherited Mum's artistic gene. "What's your story then?" Ruby questions, one felt tip in her mouth and another busily scribbling away.

"My story?"

"Yes. Is it your mum?"

I cough, still struggling with the honesty these meetings bring. "Yes. She's been diagnosed with depression, anxiety, and post-traumatic stress disorder which meant she was too scared to leave the house for most of my childhood, but she's managing it much better these days."

Evidently, I'm not.

She leans back in her chair and squints at me. "That sounds tough. Your dad? How does he cope? I sometimes think it's harder on my dad than my mum, which is silly really. He's not the one dying of cancer!"

I freeze. For so long that single word, *dad*, was a beacon of hope for me, now it makes the hairs on the back of my neck stand on end. "I don't have a dad."

"Time's up artists!" I'm grateful for Glenn's interruption. "Now show each other your masterpieces." We lift our paper, show each other our creations, and burst out laughing. Andy Warhol can rest peacefully in his grave. "Where's my neck?" I splutter.

"Never mind your neck! What about my nose? Please tell

me it's not that big!" She feels her nose with her fingers and sticks out her bottom lip.

"It's not! Turns out, I was channelling Picasso!" We laugh loudly and it feels good, maybe Glenn was right about these activities.

"Back to the circle now," he instructs. Once we're all back in a group, Glenn asks what we hope to achieve this month. George grunts a simple *dunno*, Katie wants the party to be *the best*, Frankie wants to stop attending these *pathetic meetings* and when it comes to me, I have a moment of confidence. On cue, my cheeks flare up, but I tell this small, mismatched group that I want to audition for a talent show and hopefully have a chance at gaining a scholarship for a prestigious drama school in the city.

"Ha! You on stage? You can't even speak to this group without your face blowing up like a big, fat raspberry." Frankie laughs and my cheeks let me down by turning crimson. "How are you ever going to be on stage?"

Glenn leans forward to interject, but Ruby gets in first. "Not true!" She winks at me. "If you want to be on stage, you go for it." She looks at Frankie, who's scowling. "Don't you think our lives are depressing enough? At least he has a dream. It would be a more miserable life if we didn't have dreams. What do you want to do, eh? Curse some more? Humiliate people a little bit more?" Frankie's eyes narrow and Glenn shuffles in his seat, quickly calling the meeting to a close.

Ruby and I help Glenn stack up the chairs and we walk out of the centre together. "Thanks for that back there. You know? With Frankie. She's not that bad. Just angry at the life she's been given. I think me and my tomato cheeks can fight our own battles but it's much appreciated."

"Don't mention it. Imagine if someone laughed at Martin Luther King? Imagine if he stood on stage and proudly announced to his congregation, I have a dream and then some heckler from the crowd shouted sit your arse down Marty, you talkin' nonsense!" We laugh as a silver car pulls into the carpark with three young faces pressed up against the window. "That's me. See you at the next meeting, Elliot. Remember!" She shouts and waves, "Dream big, my friend!"

I walk home through the village centre and stop off at Tom's who lives two doors down from me. He's playing a record on his old player in the living room. He stops it when I walk in. "I didn't even know that old thing worked. Don't stop for me. It sounded lovely."

He carefully takes the record off the player and puts it back in the sleeve. "This song is a classic, son. It's called "The Rose" by Bette Midler. It was Edna's favourite. We would play it every day and I would call her my peach rose." He wipes his glasses with a small cloth from his pocket.

Collapsing onto his settee, I put a cushion on my lap. "Please play it again. I would like to listen to it."

"Really?" I nod eagerly. He places it back on the player and we both listen. Tom's soon lost in memories. "Every anniversary I would go to the florists in the village and buy the biggest bunch of peach roses you've ever seen. Even now, I take some up to her grave. It's silly really." He stops the music. "Let's not feel sorry for ourselves tonight, son. Fancy tea and a custard cream?"

"Thought you would never ask." I walk over and kiss him on the cheek.

We sit and drink our brews and eat our biscuits. The cherry blossom tree in the garden opposite is full of billowy pink and white flowers, like a large cloud of candyfloss. Tom taught me about cherry blossoms when I was younger, he explained how they're Japan's national flower and symbolise renewal and hope. The television is on but the sound is turned down, a nature documentary about a herd of elephants. "It was really embarrassing at the meeting tonight, Tom. Every time Glenn asked me to speak, my cheeks set on fire and the more I tried to stop it, the hotter they got! Frankie? That girl I told you about. The angry one. She made a comment that I would never be on stage but there was a new girl there tonight, Ruby, and she shut her up so quickly." We watch as the mum elephant finally finds her lost baby elephant.

"I like the sound of this Ruby girl. You can be anything you want, son." He puts his empty mug down on the table by his chair. "Life's too short for doubt. So, your cheeks go red, imagine that feeling if you *do* manage it? Don't forget I saw you in Oliver last year. Best orphan I ever saw!"

I lean back on the settee and cross my legs. "You're biased. You've always been my biggest fan, but can I tell you something?"

He looks over. "Always."

"My drama teacher wants me to apply for a course in the city. A fancy one. They offer a scholarship if I can prove I'm good enough, so I've put myself forward for a talent show. The audition is on Monday." My eyes widen. "I'm nervous though and I've prepared nothing." He looks at a photo of him and Edna above the fireplace, taken at the Louvre in Paris. "Are you okay, Tom? You seem a bit … sad tonight."

His eyes stay fixed on the photo. "Funny how grief works. Creeps up when you least expect it. I'm just feeling it a bit tonight, son."

I nod to the photo. "Tell me about that place again then."

He laughs. "I've told you many times! You don't need an old codger like me boring you with my tales of the past."

I grin. "I do need that. One more time, please."

He smiles. "If I must. It was our favourite place. Tuileries Gardens at the Louvre. It's where I got down on one knee and asked Edna to be my wife. I promised to take her back for our fortieth wedding anniversary but … well, that never happened. It's a beautiful place, son. I remember a sea of red poppies that day and Edna especially loved the statues. I wish you could visit. I think you'd love it."

"Yeah?"

"It has some of the finest art you'll ever see. Edna loved this one piece." He scratches his head. "I can't for the life of me remember what it was called. This brain needs more oil ... The Lace Maker by Johannes Vermeer!" he shouts and laughs. "That was it! She wouldn't stop talking about it, even reading a book inspired by it. Maybe I can take you one day before I get too old, and these legs stop working?"

I go over and kiss him on the cheek. "I would love that."

He shakes his head. "Enough living in the past. Talent show auditions? Do you need a song? Maybe one you can play on the guitar. You're improving! I can teach you one of the first songs I learnt to play at college, Brown Eyed Girl by Van Morrison. When Edna and I first started courting, I would get my beloved Gibson out and play that for her."

"Seeing as I have absolutely nothing else. Brown Eyed Girl it is!"

He smiles. "Sure. Fetch my guitar from upstairs. We will work on the basic finger positioning again. Just the simple riffs. You'll be an expert in no time."

CHAPTER SEVEN

JOSH

"He turned up!" Freddie jumps off the swing, a bottle of beer in one of his hands. Two older boys I don't recognise appear next to him, both holding a cig and a bottle of beer. "Macca? Speno?" He gestures to me. "This is Josh. Someone I know from school. Don't worry. He can be trusted."

They nod their heads at me and start walking towards the skate ramp, I presume that's a sign for me to follow and I jog behind like a pathetic lapdog. What am I doing here? I told Mum I was going to Elliot's to revise for our exams, she seemed happy that I hadn't let the meeting with Marshall yesterday get me down too much. A crate of beer's hidden under the ramp, Freddie reaches down and takes two, handing one over to me. I take it even though I haven't drank since being in Cruxby with Elliot and waking up on a park bench, but something tells me not to say no to Freddie Rothwell. The three of them climb up the skate ramp and sit at the top, opening their beers on the edge of the metal platform and start talking about people I don't know and by the sounds of it ... I don't want to know. Someone called Steffan was in a car chase and caught by the police in Farnham last night. I take a swig of the beer. It's disgusting. It tastes like armpits. Why did Steve like this so much? But I swallow it down without pulling a face.

Why *am* I here?

I want to be back home with Coral and Saff, reading tales of Biff and Kipper or watching Eastenders with Mum. My phone beeps. It'll be Mum. Since Steve and Cruxby, she's become more anxious when I'm out on my own but then again, since she thinks I'll turn out like Steve ... so best not to let her down. I take another swig and start to climb the ramp, my foot slips and I spill some beer. They laugh. Eventually, I make it to the top and sit next to Freddie, take another swig and try to join in the conversation.

"I was wasted last night."

"Tommy says he can get it cheaper in Farnham."

"This is good stuff. I swear."

I nod but I don't belong here. "So, Josh." Freddie looks my way and the others smile. "We've been chatting, and we might need some help from you."

"What kind of help?" I take another sip of beer and cough.

Macca and Speno laugh. "Where did you get this one from? I think he would be better tucked up in bed with a cup of hot milk and chocolate chip cookies."

"Ignore them. They don't see what I see." He puts an arm around my shoulder. "We need some help getting some ... stuff into school. That's all. I pass you something and you pass it on to someone else. Easy. Nothing to it. Do you reckon you can do that?" His eyes narrow.

I shake my head. "I can't. I can't get into any more trouble. I made a promise."

He squeezes my shoulder. "It will be one time. We promise. Don't we lads? One favour. That's all we're asking.

We wouldn't get you in trouble." They nod and smile. "We'll make it worth your while."

"Why can't you do it?" I stutter. What fool do they take me for? I know what they want me to pass on and it will not be sweets from Mr Peters' shop. I've heard the rumours about Freddie and how he lives up at the caravan park where there's a drug raid every other month.

"Cause, my friend, Mr Owen watches my every move. Created a bit of a track record for myself, haven't I?" Macca pulls out some rizlas and places them on his knee whilst Freddie's grip tightens. "Promise. It's not serious stuff. I wouldn't do that to you. I can tell you're someone to respect." Macca pulls something from his pocket and crumbles it onto the tobacco, before rolling it up. I don't want to be here.

"Freddie. I can't. I can't do it to my mum–"

"Crap! Look lively everyone! I think we've got visitors!" Speno jumps up and hits Macca's shoulder. There's a bright light in the distance that's getting bigger, someone's walking towards us. We all jump up.

"Hold this." Macca puts the joint in my hand and the three of them jump off the ramp and run. A police officer chases them into the trees.

"Oi!" I shout, squinting as another police officer walks up to the ramp and points the torch directly in my face.

"Now then!" a deep voice comes from below. He looks up at me. He's tall and skinny with blond hair. I recognise him from coming into school and doing a talk about water safety. He shines a torch on my hand. "What do we have there?"

CHAPTER EIGHT

ELLIOT

Felicity squeezes my hand which momentarily distracts me from the anxiety bubbling away like a volcano inside my stomach. I stare at the double doors to the drama studio. It's Monday which means talent show auditions. I spent most of the weekend at Tom's, practising the song. I've still a lot to learn with the guitar but I've learnt the basic chords and the lyrics. Josh messaged me to say he got into serious trouble on Friday and his Mum has grounded him till he's thirty. I told him to find me at lunch.

I look over at Felicity. "Can we give it five minutes? I promise I won't chicken out, but can we wait five more minutes?"

She smiles. "Of course. Look at Beyonce! She always makes her audiences wait." We sit down, cross-legged, on the floor of the corridor, our backs up against the wall. "You okay, Bieber?"

"Yeah. It's anxiety. Mrs Spencer says I have *anxiety*, either that or the chicken casserole I had last night is disagreeing with me!"

She squeezes my hand again and we watch other students

tumble out of the doors talking excitedly about their successful auditions. Resting her head on my shoulder, the knot in my stomach loosens. Noise and excitement resonate through the walls of the drama studio, hopeful dancers and actors practising their high kicks and high notes.

"Anxiety?" Felicity looks over. "Because of what you've been through with your mum or born with it?"

I shrug. "I've no idea. I'm trying to cope with it and not let it ruin my life, but this ..."—I gesture to the drama studio—"is my nemesis. Think Superman and his kryptonite. Don't get me wrong, I love singing but my body has other ideas when I get up on stage, and I can't seem to control it."

"What makes you so nervous, Superman?"

My head rests on the wall behind. "It's hard to explain."

"Try."

"Well ... I've my normal nerves which have been with me all my life and hard to control, red cheeks, heart exploding out my chest but, Mr Kay's now dropped this drama course seed in my head and it's lurking there, and I'd be lying if I wasn't a tiny bit excited."

"You *are* allowed to be excited."

"I know, but we don't have the money. I would *have* to get the scholarship to be able to go. There's no way we can afford the drama course."

She stares at the floor. "I might have the money, but I do *not* have daddy's permission. You put a lot of pressure on yourself." She looks up at me. "But I know you can do this."

We stare at each other, and I desperately want to kiss her. "Before I forget, I have something for you." I unzip my briefcase and take out a book. "Sydney reserved it for me at the library."

I hand her a copy of *Fahrenheit 451*. "You remembered!" She takes the book and mouths the words of the blurb to herself. Once finished, she grabs my hand. "Thank you. That's really sweet. Now, come on! We need to be on the other side of that door before lunch finishes." She stands up and reaches for my hand. "Come on Bieber! Now or never."

"I'll opt for never, please."

"Come on!"

"This isn't going to go well."

As we walk through the doors, the drama studio's been set out like a low budget talent show you might see on Saturday night television. A line of nervous pupils sit by the wall, some with song sheets, one with a football and another messing with a row of coloured handkerchiefs. The stage is bare except for a single microphone and a small collection of instruments, and there's a desk in front of the stage where Mr Kay, Mrs Stephens and Miss Burns are sitting, chewing their pens, and looking thoughtful. A boy from the year ten football team steps up onto the stage and explains he's going to do as many keepie uppies as he can in sixty seconds. Felicity and I scuttle across to the line of chairs and take a seat. She looks over her monologue one last time.

"Albertaceratops, Allosaurus, Barasaurus, Centrosaurus--"

"Elliot!" She whispers loudly. "What are you doing?"

I look blankly at her. "Sorry."

"You were ... You were muttering some names, like dinosaurs."

My cheeks flush. "A nasty habit of mine when the bullying was bad. I would recite lists to myself like it would give me an invisible forcefield. Ignore me."

Her face brightens. "I try but you're actually hard to ignore, Elliot Hart."

Closing my eyes, I remind myself of the breathing techniques Mrs Spencer and Glenn have taught me: count in for six, hold for two, breathe out for four, count in for six. The football player finishes in style and kicks the ball over the teachers' heads hitting the wall at the back of the studio with a loud thud which is soon followed by a health and safety lecture from Mr Kay.

"Elliot?" Felicity nudges me.

"Yes?"

"You *can* do this." I open one eye and give a weak thumbs up. "You *can* do this." She repeats. I want to agree with her, like a boxer receiving a motivational speech off his coach before entering the ring. Yes, I can do this! I can get up on that stage, on my own, in front of all these people and sing a song without turning a dark shade of red or losing my voice. I want to tell her I'll be fine, but my voice has packed up and gone on holiday, so I give a weak nod instead. I'm the boxer that has been beaten to a pulp and lying in a crumpled mess in the corner of the ring whilst people point and laugh. Slowly, the line of auditionees whittles down, as we watch hopeful pupil after hopeful pupil take their turn. A group of year seven girls prance up to the stage in their PE kits and proudly announce they will be doing a dance to the Pussycat Dolls, one of the girls is always a step behind the others and keeps getting shouted at. Mr Kay and his entourage give little away, merely giving each expectant auditionee a simple *thank you* or *next*. After each audition, they have a hushed conversation and scribble on their paper. It's starting to feel slightly like I'm under water, voices around me are becoming muffled. I close my eyes again and picture Mum in the kitchen, smiling, nodding her head to tell me you're good enough and you can do this.

I can do this.

Another technique Glenn has taught me when anxiety ploughs into me like a dumper truck is visualising a successful outcome. I push the image of me as a defeated boxer out of my mind and try to replace it with someone who sings confidently and effortlessly, but each time I try to picture this maestro, I see me, standing on that damn stage frozen, unable to utter a word or move. I look at Felicity, panicked.

I can't do this.

"Elliot Hart!" The trio of judges look my way. I keep my eyes on Felicity, she smiles, but I shake my head.

I can't do this.

"Go on." Felicity nudges me off my chair. There's only three of us left to audition but there are lots of shadows at the back of the room, lurkers, ready to watch the comical Elliot Hart Show. I feel sick. "Go on!" There's an urgency to her voice now. I'm embarrassing her. I'm embarrassing myself.

I can do this.

A more determined voice in my head. A voice I kind of recognise. The voice who helped me deliver a speech in history or sing Hallelujah with the busker in Cruxby. The voice who got me out of bed each day when Mum was sick. I stand up and take the walk of death, two wooden steps, onto the stage.

Mr Kay starts, "What will you be performing for us today?"

"I'll be singing Brown Eyed Girl by Van Morrison. Do you have a guitar I could borrow, Sir?" My voice is wobbling. Felicity has her hands clasped together and nods eagerly. The lurkers laugh.

"Yes, of course. By the side of the stage and great song choice by the way." He claps his hands together. "When you're ready, off you go."

I walk over to the edge of the stage and grab a guitar; it looks different to Tom's Gibson at home. My heart's racing fast. I wonder if those at the back of the room can hear it. I've rehearsed these lyrics, even Mum said I was singing them in my sleep. Everyone's quiet and staring. The sound of my heavy breathing echoes down the microphone and even that stops for a mini second. Breathe Elliot, for God's sake remember to breathe. If anything, at least remember to breathe. The doors to the drama studio open and everyone looks towards them, Josh walks in, leans on the wall, folds his arms and smiles at me. I relax a little and smile back, take one last deep breath, put the guitar strap over my neck and start playing. Once comfortable with the chords, I start singing. My voice sounds okay, decent. It's confident, clear. I visualise myself in Cruxby, with the busker, with Josh, by the fountain. I picture the old ladies smiling and clapping. I can see Josh punching the air when I finished the song. I stand taller, smile, and remember each word.

I can do this.

But then just as suddenly, I'm not at the fountain anymore.

I'm outside the pub, with the girl with red fingernails, she's telling me Gavin's in jail. She's saying the man we thought would save us is serving time for sexual assault. I've realised my mum was his victim. Why am I here? Go back to the fountain, go to your kitchen, go anywhere but here.

Be in this room.

Be present.

Sing the next line.

I trip up on the next words, forget the next chord and try to start it again. *He sexually assaulted two women*. Me crying, hitting Josh. I've forgotten the next line. I've no words. The guitar hangs heavy around my neck.

Sniggers.

Whispers.

Laughs.

Mrs Stephens and Miss Burns simultaneously lean forward, willing me to not give up but I can't remember what to sing. My mind's blank. I let go of the guitar.

I'm done.

I'll not get in the talent show and I'll not get the

scholarship. It's only then I realise my heart's racing, my hands are shaking, and my eyes are filling up.

"Elliot. You can finish now. Come off the stage please." Mrs Stephens stands and I hope she isn't going to come over and give me a hug.

"Matchstick! Another priceless performance!"

"Booooooo!"

"Look at him! He looks like he's going to cry!"

"Shut it." Josh grabs one of the hecklers and pushes him into the wall before running over and hopping on to the stage, taking the guitar off me and placing it gently on the floor, he grabs my elbow. "Personally, I thought you smashed it, but this is our cue to leave." He grins and half drags me out of the studio, whilst Mr Kay calls Felicity up to the stage. Once out of the room, I lean against the wall and slowly crouch down, putting my head in between my knees. Josh stands near me.

He laughs. "I think that went very well."

"Oh God! What's up with me?" I look up to Josh. "Why can't I stand up on a stage and sing? When I sing at home, with Tom, even in class, I feel like me. It is the only time I feel truly like me. You remember Cruxby? The busker?" I pathetically plead for reassurance, but I need to know that I'm not making this up. I need to know I'm not chasing an impossible dream. "How can I ever get a scholarship, if I can't perform on a stage?"

He smiles and nods. "You were great in Cruxby. I knew then that I had been there when Elliot Hart was first discovered but you might need to work on those nerves a touch."

"You think?" Memories of the last ten minutes swirl in my head. "That was utterly humiliating!" I put my head back in my hands and groan. Josh grabs my arm and heaves me up. "Come on, let's get out of here and honestly, it wasn't that bad." He laughs and I stare at him. "Okay, it was pretty excruciating but if it makes you feel better, maybe not as humiliating as that briefcase you're carrying around!"

We walk down the corridor together. "You okay?" I ask. "What happened on Friday?"

"I'll tell you about it later."

"Josh?" I grab his arm and he faces me. "What is it? What's happened? What have you done?"

"Nothing! I'm fine. I promise. I'll tell you later. Let's focus on your drama for now."

"Okay. Well, I blame this brain. I've no control over it. So, there I am on stage trying to show everyone that I can do this and for some reason, my stupid brain takes me back to the pub in Cruxby, that woman in the bar, with the red nails, you—"

"Look," Josh interrupts. Freddie Rothwell's leaning by the wall ahead of us, staring at Josh and gesturing for him to come over. "I need to speak to that rat, but we'll chat later. I want to talk about stupid brains too but do not overthink this! We'll think of something."

"But overthinking is my forte!" I look at Freddie. He terrifies me. Out of everyone in the school, he scares me the most. Some say he broke someone's nose for wearing the same colour T-shirt as him. "Josh! You promised your mum that you would stay out of trouble."

"Bit late for that actually but don't worry about me I've got him sorted and don't sweat the audition." He runs off shouting, "We've been through much worse!"

CHAPTER NINE

JOSH

"You do know that you can't be mad at me forever, don't you Mum?" Ever since the police officer drove me home last Friday evening and lectured me and my mum about the dangers of cannabis, she's given me the silent treatment. Three whole days of silence. She grabs a tea towel and starts drying the plates, throwing each one into the kitchen cupboard. "Mum! I've said I'm sorry like a trillion times. This boy, Macca, put the joint into my hand. I've never smoked weed and never will." She slams a plate down and places both hands on the kitchen counter, leaning forward. She won't look at me. "It doesn't matter what I say, does it? I know what you think."

She spins. "You do? Do you?"

"Yes."

"You have no idea what I think."

"I do!"

Her eyes narrow. "I'll tell you what I think. I think my sixteen year old son was brought home by the police for being in possession of a class B drug. You're lucky you got off with a warning. You can wave goodbye to any ideas of getting into joinery college with a criminal record. There you go! That's what I think. Happy?"

"Nope. That's not all of it. There's something else you think."

"Is there?"

"Yes. Something you won't say to me but quite happy to share with others."

She rubs her forehead. "Please enlighten me. I'm dying to know."

"You think ..." She stares at me. "You think I'll turn out like Steve."

She continues to look at me, before placing the tea towel down and slowly walking over, taking a seat and grabbing my hand. "You need to listen to me very carefully. Are you listening?" I nod. "You are *nothing* like Steve. Do you hear me? Nothing. Not one bit."

"Don't lie!" I shout. "You don't believe that. I heard you say it."

She lets go of my hand and stands. "What? When?"

"Last Tuesday, when I walked Coral home from school, you were on the phone to Vee."

"Really? Then? That's what all this is about?" She throws her hands in the air. "I was angry! Worried. Upset. I had just listened to a voice message saying you had shouted at another pupil and stormed out of the class." She sits back down. "I didn't–I don't–I don't think you are like him but yes, I'm worried. I'm worried about—"

"About what? That I'll hurt others?"

"No." She shakes her head and sits. "Not at all. I'm worried *I've* messed you up. Never mind the Steves in the world, it's *me* who messed all this up for you. The only role models you've had in your life are men like him. This is all *my* fault, not yours."

I grab her hand. "It isn't. They're not my role models.

They're my anti-role models." She smiles. "You. *You* are my role model. I want to be more like you."

"What a tired, grumpy single mum who upsets her son?"

"You've raised three children by yourself. You've left an abusive man and set up a whole new life. It's me! It's *my* fault. I make bad choices. I've told Freddie I don't want anything to do with him."

"How did he take that?"

"Didn't look too pleased."

"Freddie's not the kind of person to be hanging around with."

"I know."

My phone beeps. It's Elliot.

Walk to school? Meet in the park?

I lean over and kiss her on the forehead. "Let's leave it there and stop blaming ourselves. No more trouble. Promise. I'm going to go." I stand up and grab my school bag.

She looks at her watch. "But school doesn't start for half an hour."

"I'm going to meet Elliot."

Sitting on the metal bench at the park, I watch a dad help his young son climb to the top of the rope tower, placing a hand on his leg when he needs it but then letting go and praising him when he manages to take a tentative step on his own. The dad's arms remain open wide, ready to catch his son at any point. This park's not changed since I was a boy. There's still the really tall metal slide that gives you friction burns on your arse every time you slide down and would send any health and safety inspector into a major panic attack. Next to it is an old rusty roundabout and the metal horse with most of the paint peeling off. There's also the sandpit that I'm sure is hiding a nice collection of cigarette butts and broken beer bottles. Me and the girls come here, playing hide and seek in the overgrown blackberry bushes or me pushing them high on the swings.

Elliot walks up the path. "Good morning." He sits down, and we watch the same dad take his son over to the swings. "What happened last weekend? I overheard Anusha at tutor time, and she said they found drugs on you," he says gently, avoiding looking at me. He's changed since our trip to Cruxby, taller, hair shorter and even some stubble sprouting on his chin.

"I met up with Freddie and some older lads here on Friday. One of them put a joint in my hand and a policeman turned up and took me home."

"Josh!"

"I know! Please don't lecture me. Mum's made me feel awful. I've told Freddie to leave me alone, said I didn't give the police his name and he owes me one, but I don't think he cares about anyone but himself. He still wants me to take some stuff into school for him."

"Stuff?"

"Yes, *stuff*."

"You can't, Josh. You need to avoid him. He's not the kind of person to be hanging around with. His dad's in prison!"

"So is ours!"

He laughs. "Fair point. But you know what I mean."

"I know. Why does trouble have a habit of finding me?"

Eddie Rain, a homeless man I met last year when I ran away from home, staggers up the path carrying his sleeping bag under his arm. He smiles, his teeth yellow or missing. "Good morning, Josh. How are you today?"

"I'm okay. You? Need anything?"

He smiles wider, exposing more gaps. "Don't you worry about me. I'm grand. Got everything I need here." He slaps his sleeping bag. "But thank you for asking." He nods to us both and walks off down the path.

Elliot looks confused. "How do you know him?"

"Eddie? I met him the night before our trip to Cruxby, remember? He's the guy who gave me that bottle of whiskey we both enjoyed. I try to check in on him every now and again."

Elliot looks over and smiles. We sit in silence and watch the park fill with younger children in their uniforms on their way to school. "What else is it, Josh? It's not just delightful Freddie Rothwell. There's more to it. The outburst in English? Why do you let Lewis get to you? What—"

"I'm going to fail my exams," I interrupt.

"You don't know that—"

"I do! And if I don't pass Maths *and* English, I can't get into the joinery course at college. The only thing I'm good at is cutting up wood."

"And checking in on the homeless and looking after your sisters and looking after your mum and shouting at people who take the piss out of me. But yes, all you're good at is *cutting up wood*." He rolls his eyes.

I laugh. "You're my brother. You're biased." I look to the sky. "I've tried so hard this past year, tried to keep out of trouble, avoided Lewis, helped with the girls so Mum could keep her job and why?" I fling my arms in the air. "It was all a complete waste of time. Once a disappointment, always a disappointment."

"No, you—"

"Do you know Marshall called my mum into school?" Elliot shakes his head. "They think I'm stupid and want to test me so they have physical evidence that I *am* stupid. Dyslexia or something."

"Dyslexia doesn't mean you're stupid." Elliot messes with the lid of his water bottle, clearly choosing his words carefully.

"I've read about dyslexia. It's when the brain works differently that's all and it doesn't have anything to do with your intelligence, it—"

"Say what you want. To me? It's saying I'm stupid but simply putting a fancy label on it. A label I probably wouldn't be able to read." I force a smile.

"No," he states. "Not at all. Everyone must get from A to B and your brain takes a different route that's all. That's how I understood it." A gaggle of shrieking children race in front of us playing a game of What Time is it Mr Wolf? "Do you know what you said to me in Cruxby? Something I've always remembered." I shrug. "You told me to start asking for help. You told me to stop being so stubborn and scared and ask for help. I'm doing it! I attend young carers' meetings every month. If Mr Marshall's offering help, accept it. So what, you might have dyslexia, you've always been one of a kind Josh McBride! You were born different."

"What I'm getting from you here is you think I *should* take the test?"

"See! And you call yourself stupid!" He takes a gulp of water. "Yes. Take the test."

"I'll think about taking the test on one condition." Elliot looks over. "That audition you utterly bombed at?"

"I wouldn't say *utterly bombed*."

"Ha! Okay then, that audition you *kind of* bombed at." I laugh. "I'll take the test if you find Mr Kay and ask if you can do the audition again. Remember? I was there in Cruxby when you left the whole of the town square speechless. You're really good at singing. Give it one more try, and I promise I'll think about the dyslexia screening."

We stand up and Elliot offers me a hand. "Deal. Let's get going before we're both late for school."

———

"We'll look over the periodic table one more time." Science, like Maths, is another subject that *sets* its pupils. The teachers believe it's good for us to be constantly reminded if we are bright or stupid, even better when they put a number next to it, so we don't forget. Maybe they think it's character building. I'm in set four, the bottom set, for both Maths and Science. Like Maths, it's a smaller group and seems to be filled with teenagers who have their own personal assistant and some who have zero interest in learning. Zane Aitken spends the full hour turning on the gas tap when Sir's back is turned, and until my trip to Cruxby with Elliot, I would've been helping him. I've tried this year. I'm okay when it comes to the practical experiments, but a lot of marks go to the writing part. Sir's given up a couple of his lunchtimes to help me, but it seems I'm a lost cause and have a season pass for set four.

"Is everyone listening?" Mr Gregson stands at the front, always smartly dressed in a tweed waistcoat and white shirt, like he was meant to be going to the day at Cruxby races but took a wrong turn and found himself here with us *troublesome lot*. "Look at the sheet in front of you and decide which element they are. Then—" The phone in the classroom rings and everyone falls silent, even Charlie stops throwing chewed up pieces of paper at poor Gabby sitting in front of him. Each one of us thinks the phone call is for them. We all, simultaneously, cast our minds back over the day's and week's events to see if there's anything that would warrant a phone call from the headmaster. I run over the morning's events to reassure myself I've stayed out of trouble. Sir walks over to his desk and picks up the phone. "Hello. Yes? Josh McBride?" The class turns and stares at me.

Me?

Have the police been in touch? Has Freddie got me in trouble? He's pissed off that I'm ignoring his messages. "You're wanted at the Learning Support Department, Josh."

He puts the phone down and strides over to my table. "Nothing to worry about," he whispers. "A screening they want you to do. They said to take your bag as it might go into lunch." Great. Time to answer lots of questions to prove I'm stupid. I collect my bag and walk down the corridor, already deciding to *not* go to the learning support department but hide at the oak tree instead until the bell rings for lunch, but I want to avoid Freddie. If Mum asks, I'll say I didn't get the message. I can't think of anything worse than sitting opposite someone who pats my head and smiles whilst watching me fail every soddin' question they ask.

"Josh!" Elliot comes running up the corridor, slightly out of breath, his briefcase swinging by his side.

"Hey." We smile at each other and fall into a comfortable silence for a second or two. A comfortableness I don't think I get with anyone else, not even Mum, as she's always *off to work* or in the *middle of something*. "Why are *you* out of class? I thought you would get an allergic reaction to missing valuable lesson time."

He smiles. "Funny. Just doing an errand for Mrs Stephens."

"Have you asked Mr Kay for another audition yet?"

"No, I saw him this morning and I was going to ask but— but—" he looks down at his shoes.

"But? But?"

"But ... I'm terrified. I can't humiliate myself like that again and even if he does say yes, and I do manage to get through it, there's no chance I'm getting in the show, what's the point of putting myself through this again?" He hangs his head.

"No." The loudness of my voice startles us both and he looks up. "No. No. No." I shake my head vigorously with each word. "We didn't take our sorry arses to Cruxby, get mugged, sing with a busker, annoy an Irish cook and find out our dad is a … we didn't do all that to be standing in this corridor, still … scared little boys. No." My voice echoes down the empty corridor. "You damn well will ask for that audition even if I have to drag you there myself! Not because you might get into some fancy la de dah drama college but to prove to yourself that you *can* do it."

Elliot bursts out laughing and puts his hands up in mock surrender. "Okay! Chill!" We walk down the corridor, and he looks my way. "It's called Cruxby Royal College of Arts and not la de dah drama college by the way." He smiles. "And you? Where are you off to? Don't dare tell me you're off to meet Freddie."

"No!" I stop and face him. "I'm off for my dyslexia screening."

The Learning Support Department is a small building hidden behind the main school, surrounded by large conifer trees. It has its own yard outside with three wooden picnic benches. Walking through the entrance, I feel like a fool not knowing which room to knock on.

"Josh! Hi." Marshall comes past holding a pile of textbooks. "You look lost."

"I'm fine." I look to the floor, and he places the set of books on a filing cabinet by the wall, putting his hands in his pockets.

"Are you here for the dyslexia screening?" I nod. "Good. Look at me, Josh." I raise my head up and look over his shoulder. "You're a bright boy. I hear some of the ideas you have in class when you're chatting with those around you, and you're spot on. Really insightful! It's important we see if you need some extra support getting all those ideas down on paper. That's it." I stay quiet. "I know I'm on your case a lot. I do. I know I nag at you and tell you off sometimes, but surely that's better than ignoring you. Not caring. Letting you do what you want. I believe you can do this." He picks up the books and starts to head off before turning around. "Some might say it's time you started believing in yourself."

"Josh?" A young woman, early twenties, wearing a white T-shirt and black dungarees appears behind me. I nod. "Come with me."

I follow her into a small room with four small desks and chairs. There are cheesy motivational posters pinned up on the wall, telling me *You are the artist of your own life* and *Don't hand the paintbrush to anyone else,* and *Today is the opportunity to build the tomorrow you want.* The woman introduces herself as Nina and explains her job is to see if I need extra support at school and, if needed, refer me to a dyslexia specialist. "Take a seat Josh." She sits and organises some sheets of paper in front of her. My hands feel sweaty, exactly like I feel before an assessment in class. "Now, nothing to worry about. This won't take long. We're going to have a little chat about how you're finding your schoolwork and then I'll get you to read a few words to me." I look over her shoulder at the trees on the hillside, standing in a line like soldiers ready to battle. "Is that okay?" I nod, again. "Good. Can you explain to me, in your own words, what it is like in lessons? Maybe, think back to the assessments you've had and try to tell me what it feels like from *your* perspective."

I think back to all the years at school I've spent struggling, disappointing everyone, and getting into trouble. "People think I'm lazy," I mutter, tearing at one of my fingernails and unable to look her in the eye. "People think I'm lazy or that I'm not trying but it's not true. I work hard every bloody day." I stop and she smiles, gesturing for me to carry on. "I'm trying hard, but it doesn't seem to make any difference y'know? I can listen to the teachers, but I don't seem to get it like the others in the class get it. It takes me longer and then if it's an exam or something, the timer runs out and I'm not finished and the teachers look at me with that face, y'know? A mixture of pity and frustration." She smiles, nods and scribbles on the paper in front of her. It's an odd relief for someone to ask what it is like for me at school. I'm not sure anyone has ever directly asked me that before.

"What do you enjoy about school?"

"There's a part of school I enjoy. P.E is fine, and technology is good. I built the best bird box in the class, and I've made some shelves and a table at home. I'm in the middle of making something for my mum, but then there are parts of school I dread, hate even, like reading aloud in class or even sometimes, knowing my times table. My school life seems filled with embarrassing read-alouds, missed homeworks, detentions and getting into trouble. Teachers can teach me stuff and it doesn't seem to stay in my brain."

She smiles and continues writing notes. "It seems to me that you've a different way of learning to everyone else."

"I've diagnosed myself."

"Have you?" She smiles. "Do tell?"

"Yes. I've a dud brain gene. I can spell a word correctly one day and then like that," I click my fingers. "I spell it differently the next day!"

"How does all this make you feel?" I think back to all the times Steve called me retarded and worthless.

"Like I'm stupid. That people will find out I'm stupid, but the worse—" I stop, keep my eyes on the trees. "Like I'm disappointing everyone. There's this look I get from my mum and Marshall ... Mr Marshall, it looks like they want to help me, but they're really frustrated at me too, like I'm doing it on purpose but I'm not!"

She puts her pen down. "I'm sure they aren't mad at you. They probably don't realise how hard it is for you each day and they probably don't know how to support you. You need to explain to them what it feels like."

"Maybe. But I can't see how anyone can help me except operate on my brain!"

"I'll put my scalpel away, shall I? No operations today, sorry." She leans back on her chair and smiles. "But we can start from being in this room right now. We can see if there's a dyslexia diagnosis and then go from there. Does that sound okay to you?"

I shrug. "Suppose."

She grabs a handful of cards from her bag. "Good, and mark my words, Josh McBride. You're *not* stupid, lazy, or worthless."

CHAPTER TEN

ELLIOT

"Tell me again, how learning to dance will cure my mum's cancer? All this money going into research, and you're trying to tell me the secret to curing cancer is actually foxtrotting around Mallowbank Community Centre!" Ruby laughs.

"Shush! I'm concentrating!" I wipe my hand on my jeans and grab Ruby's left hand, unsure what to do with my other hand as it flaps around like a fish until Ruby forces it onto her hip. Glenn's booked a dance instructor, Dancing Dan, for this Friday's young carer session. I have to agree with Ruby, I'm not sure how learning to tango solves our problems because it's simply highlighting more of them, like my two left feet! But Glenn started the meeting with a passionate speech about forgetting our worries, loosening up and having fun, but being this close to a girl is doing anything but *loosening up,* and I don't need Dancing Dan to prove how little coordination I have.

"Ouch!" Ruby winces as I stand on her toe ... again.

"Follow my lead," she implores. "It's easy, one, two, three, four, and then you move back one, two and forward—" She throws me around the community centre whilst I show the sophistication of a drunk giraffe. "Let me get this straight, you froze on stage? No words came out at all?" She grimaces. "And Felicity was there too? That girl you like?" Dancing Dan shouts something in Spanish and shakes his hips. "Let's see it as a minor setback. What are we going to do about it now?"

"Hide?"

"Let's start from zee beginning!" Dan claps his hands and jumps on the spot. I'm not sure who the accent or fake tan is trying to fool. Dan's mum owns the Golden Fleece pub, and he was born and bred right here in Mallowbank. "Thiz time? Really feeeeel the music." The music begins, Dan gyrates his hips and we start again.

"And what's with the *we*?" I ask Ruby. "I'm capable of messing up my life all by myself thank you very much."

She suddenly stops and holds my shoulders tight. "Put the violin away please, Mister Hart. I've better things to do on a Friday night than waltz around Mallowbank Community Centre being your agony aunt but," she throws her hands in the air, "Here I am! Now one, two—" I follow her lead and manage to successfully miss each and every step. "I think you should try again, away from other pupils and definitely away from the girl you love."

"I don't love her!" We start the routine again and smile at each other when I don't squish her feet this time. "But funnily enough, that's what Josh said I should do too."

She spins gracefully under my arm. "Josh? Who's he?"

"Have I not told you about Josh? He's ... how should I put this? He's–he's a boy who bullied me for years before running away with me to Cruxby, where I found out he was my half-brother, and our dad's in jail for sexually assaulting women, one of which was my mum sixteen years ago." There's a part of me that secretly liked shocking her with all the facts. A drunk giraffe with a dark past.

She lets go of my hand and stares, doing the maths. "Sixteen years ago?"

I smile weakly. "Yep. Voila! One sexual assault and here I am. Who doesn't love some complicated baggage, eh?"

"Holy crap. That's nuts!" I hold her hand whilst she spins around to the music, for someone who exudes so much toughness, she's very agile. "It doesn't seem fair, does it?"

"What?"

We stop. "Well, when the bad hands are being dealt, you think they should be dealt equally and fairly, but they're not. Some people seem to get all the duff hands. I'm sorry about your mum." She stares at Dancing Dan who's trying to convince George to get up off his chair.

"Oi," I grab her, and we complete the routine flawlessly. "Don't go down that dark path. No, it's not fair but we keep going, don't we? We keep putting one step forward, just like this Tango. Ha! Maybe Glenn's on to something!"

She looks at me, her face softening. "I know, but I wish that hadn't happened to your mum, and you. Are you going to listen to me and Josh? Audition again? You wouldn't put yourself through all this if it wasn't something you really wanted to do. And maybe if we *know* life can be really tough, we should work *really* hard for what we want. You only get one shot at it and all that."

"You mean I should humiliate myself again?"

The music stops and she winks. "Potato, potata."

"Maybe. One step forward, eh?"

"Yes! As long as that step doesn't land on my feet!" She laughs and the rest of the group stare. We decide to take a break and sit on the plastic chairs lining the edge of the room.

"Enough about me." I offer her a plate full of soggy Jammie Dodgers from the table. "How are things at your home?"

"Much the same." She rests her head against the window

and eats her biscuit. "Mum spends most of her time in bed, drugged up on painkillers and dad works shifts around looking after us four. Everyone seems to tell me I'm coping okay, but I think that's because I'm on survival mode, you know? I'm just getting through each day and trying not to be a total pain in the arse for my dad."

"You're allowed to be a total arse, you know? We're teenagers. It's in the contract, especially a young carer contract."

"A contract we never signed up for, eh?" Ruby rolls her eyes, and we look at each other in a way that only young carers can, a look of understanding and ... exhaustion.

Glenn calls us over to give Dancing Dan a clap for being so *generous with his time* before we are gathered back to the sharing circle to discuss our hopes for this month. George grunts, Katie hopes she will find a prom dress and Frankie wants to not fight with her mum. I'm proud of Frankie's honesty, we catch each other's eye and smile.

"Elliot?" Glenn leans forward.

"I guess–I guess–I need to finally decide what I'm doing next year." I think of the blank application form still sitting in my bag. The deadline's soon. He nods for me to elaborate but I can't forget how badly the audition went. "I'm thinking ... Farnham college and study something like maths." My shoulders sag and Ruby looks over.

We say our goodbyes and head outside into the sunshine. I wait with Ruby until her dad arrives. She looks over at me. "It's been a pleasure leading you around the dancefloor tonight, but can I be honest with you?" She tilts her head and puts her hand over her eyes to shield from the sun's glare. "Granted. I've only known you a short time but I'm calling boloney on wanting to study Maths at Farnham Community College. When you talk about singing and that drama course your eyes do this funny thing, like your pupils are actually dancing! When you mentioned Maths?" She claps her hands together. "No dancing! Eyes were dead on the dance floor!" Her dad's car pulls up and beeps. "Think about it!" She shouts as she goes to greet her gaggle of younger brothers. "We only get one shot!"

I walk back through the village square. Ruby's right, I do want to go to college in Cruxby. I want to be with people who are as passionate about singing and acting as I am. I want to study from the best and see what I am capable of, but I can't see a future where that could happen. A group of men congregate outside the Golden Fleece, holding beers, and smoking cigarettes whilst an elderly couple take a seat on the bench under the cenotaph and share a bag of chips. Walking up my street, I notice the curtains are closed at my house and all the lights are off. It's only half eight, Mum's either in bed or out, but she's never usually out at this time. A familiar feeling drums in my chest. Holding my breath, I unlock the door and find the house dark and deathly quiet. "Mum? Mum?" I check the living room, kitchen and she's not there. I race upstairs, taking two steps at once, but she's not in her bedroom either. "Mum!" My heart beats faster.

"Elliot? You home?" Mum's voice calls from downstairs. I run to the top of the stairs as she bustles through the front door holding her large art folder and rucksack. "Elliot! Hi!" She drops it all on the floor and closes the door behind her. "How are you? How was the session?"

I spin around and head for my bedroom, lie on my bed and watch the planets hanging from the ceiling. My chest still drumming. Mum's head appears around the door. "Oi. You okay?"

Turning to face the window, I look at the streetlamp opposite. She comes and sits next to me on the bed and places a hand on my leg. "I thought we were going to be honest with each other. What's up?" She holds my hand and I notice speckles of orange paint around her fingernails.

"Where were you?" I mutter.

"I told you. I had a meeting with Clint about my latest submission and I guess we got chatting. Elliot, I'm thirty-four years old, and the last I knew about it ... I don't have a curfew."

"You could've messaged me. It would've taken two seconds. The house was quiet, and I panicked." I sit up, pull my knees up tight to my chest.

She sweeps the hair from my eyes. "I thought I told you. Yes. I should've messaged. I'm sorry. I will next time. Want to see my latest piece?" Mum goes downstairs, quickly reappearing with her folder and taking a seat next to me. She unzips the folder and pulls out a large canvas. There's a young boy with orange hair sitting on a bench with a woman, both eating chips out of a paper cone.

I smile and rest my head on her shoulder. "It's us, at the cenotaph. Playing that game we made up. What was it called?"

"Name the Secret."

"Yes! That was it. I loved that game. You were always so good at it." We both stare at the painting. "Mum? Can we talk about September?"

"Of course." She carefully puts the painting back in her folder. "I was talking to Clint about Farnham college, and he says it's meant to be really good."

"Well ..." I lift my head off her shoulder and look at her. "Mr Kay thinks I've a real talent for drama, especially singing. There's a really good course at the college in Cruxby. You stay there during the week. It's expensive, but they offer two scholarships. Mr Kay thinks I could be offered one, but I have to get into the school talent show and prove I'm good enough."

"Move over." I shuffle up and she lies down next to me, pulling a notepad out from under the covers. "What's this?"

I grab it off her. "Nothing. I've just been writing a song for the talent show but it's silly. Anyway, this course?"

"It's in Cruxby?"

"Yes."

"And you have to perform solo on stage"

"Yes."

"And if you get in, you might stay there?"

"Yes."

We look out of the window. "Do you want to know what I think?"

"Yes!"

She smiles. "I think you should go for it."

———

The following Monday, I find myself in the drama studio with Mr Kay. He rolls up the sleeves of his white shirt and sits on a small stool by the piano. "Okay, Elliot. There's only me and you in the room today. Brown Eyed Girl again, yeah? It's a great song. What made you choose this one?"

"It's one of my neighbour's favourites, Sir." My voice is loud down the microphone and echoes around the empty theatre. The drama studio feels enormous. I'm too small. I slowly place my fingers around the microphone and open my mouth, but no sound comes out. The room's pressing down on me. It actually feels like the walls are moving and closing in. I'm trying every technique Mum has passed on through her CBT group, breathing around an imaginary rectangle, picturing myself singing on this stage like a famous popstar. I even try to picture a crowd in front of me, eyes wide, mouths open. Mum, Tom, Josh and Felicity in the front row, hands clasped, tears in their eyes, Mum whispering to the stranger sitting next to her, *that's my boy*, but nerves have a habit of being stronger than any top tips from a CBT class. My legs feel like they will collapse underneath me, and my hands are shaking. "No guitar today?"

"I thought I would try this audition without it, Sir. See if it helps."

"Okay. From the top, Elliot!" Sir starts to play the piano and my breath races round the imaginary rectangle like a formula one car. He pauses at my cue to start singing and nods his head in my direction, but no sound comes out.

Mute.

His pitiful look makes my voice retreat even farther down my throat, never to be seen again. Detectives in Mallowbank will forever be baffled by the mysterious case of the teenage boy's missing voice. My grip on the microphone tightens and I close my eyes, picturing myself in Tom's living room, the fire's roaring, and we're sitting together on his settee. His guitar is on my lap, and he's patiently teaching me each lyric and placing my fingers in the correct position on the strings. He smells of Pears soap. Sir starts playing again and I sway to the beat.

I start singing.

It doesn't take long for me to find the rhythm. Keeping my eyes tightly shut, I stay with Tom, and sing along with Sir's piano, we sound good together. We're already on the chorus and I'm really enjoying it – my voice is louder and more confident.

Stuff you Gavin Turner.
Stuff you anxiety.
Stuff you depression.
Stuff you Clint.

I open my eyes and smile at Sir, take the microphone out of the stand and move around the stage clicking my fingers along to the beat. My heart's racing. I don't feel small.

I feel huge!

I fill the stage!

I fit this room!

We're coming to the end; Mr Kay's off his seat and looking my way, his fingers dancing along the piano keys. His face is flushed. I can't help but laugh and belt out the final few lines before letting my voice drift softly into the air.

Silence.

The most delicious silence. A silence I want to wrap myself up in for a very long time. I know Mr Kay's staring at me, but I look to the floor and slow down my breathing, put my microphone back, place my hand in my pocket and wrap a loose thread around my finger.

"Elliot Hart! Blow me down with a feather!" He gets up off his stool and strides over to the front of the stage, looking up. "Where did that come from? I always knew you were exceptionally talented but woah!" A smile spreads across his face. "That was brilliant! That was incredible. Your voice! So unique and powerful ... I think I need to sit." He skips back over to the stool and takes a seat, running his fingers through his grey hair. "Okay, this is how I see it. You have, without a shadow of the doubt, the best voice of anyone who has ever auditioned at St. Cuthbert's."

"Really?"

"Granted, it was a shaky start but the voice, that voice!" I look up and smile. He shakes his head again and looks up to the ceiling like he's trying to solve a tricky Maths problem. "Elliot, you definitely have a place in this year's talent show!"

"Really?" I squeak. "Really? You're not kidding? Being sarcastic? Making jokes? I've been known to miss those cues in the past." I jump off the stage and jog over to him.

He stands and holds out a hand for me to shake. "Really. Come and sit with me, Elliot." We perch on the edge of the stage, our legs dangling off the edge. "Have you given any thought to the drama college? Did Mrs Spencer give you the application form?" Suddenly my high from the audition is waning. "You're really talented; your voice is incredibly unique and soulful. It would be a waste—"

"We can't afford it, Sir."

He tidies up the music sheets. "You know they offer two scholarships each year on the condition of good grades, a good reference which I can do, and watching you perform live. I'm going to invite the tutor to the talent show. If they hear what I've just heard ..." He shakes his head in disbelief. "I don't see how they can't *not* take you on."

My head's swimming. I can't believe in this future he's describing. I can't believe this could come true. *How can it?* I'm still yet to perform solo in front of an audience; I only just pulled it together today. "I don't know, Sir. You've seen what happens when I get on stage. I wouldn't want you to invite him in and I embarrass you."

He jumps off the stage. "Embarrass me? I'll rephrase it. I'm going to invite the tutor from Cruxby Royal College of Arts to the talent show and if he happens to see you perform." He claps his hands together. "What luck! Any ideas on song choice for the night? You could do this one or—"

"Well, I've actually been writing one of my own. I haven't told anyone, but if I feel brave enough on the night, I might give it a go. Is that silly?"

"No. That sounds perfect. Good things are going to happen for you, Elliot. I can feel it."

CHAPTER ELEVEN

JOSH

"Tickets go on sale for your prom tomorrow. Edward and the art committee will be selling them for five pounds each, and all proceeds will be going to a charity." Mrs Spencer announces. "Which charity is it, Edward?"

She looks over to him and his face goes red at the unexpected attention. "We haven't decided yet," his words tumble out. "We thought maybe the dog shelter, but we raised money for them last year."

Miss turns to face the class. "Well, has anyone any suggestions?"

Anusha puts her hand up. "My mum ran a race at the weekend for cancer. We could raise money for cancer research, Miss?"

"Good idea, Nush. Anyone else?"

I raise my hand half up and Miss doesn't even try to hide her surprise. "Josh?"

The rest of the group turn and stare in equal shock. "What about something for the homeless, too? There's a man who sleeps at the park who could do with some help and there's also an old woman at the station who raises money through the Big Issue. There must be some sort of charity that helps the homeless. In the city, there's a place they can go for a warm dinner. I think Mallowbank—"

"Pah!" Lewis snorts. "Waste of all our well-earned money if you ask me."

Miss glares at him. "I'm not sure anyone *did* ask you and enlighten me, what money have *you* earned Lewis?"

He ignores her. "My dad says not to give them anything. It will only fund their habits."

Miss shakes her head and rolls her eyes. "A little empathy can go a long way, Lewis. We don't know the situations that lead to people becoming homeless."

"I agree with Josh." Miss looks equally surprised when Elliot chips in. There are murmurs of agreement from others too. "People can become homeless through no fault of their own, like if their home life was too dangerous or if their parents were abusive." His cheeks go red, and he quickly looks at me and then at the table.

"Edward?" Miss asks. "What do you think? It sounds like a good idea to me. What about using the money to create a food bank? Do you want to take our ideas back to the committee and see what they say? Thanks boys." She smiles. "What great contributions ... from *most* of you." She picks up a pile of yellow cards from her desk. "Now, a little activity for today's tutor session."

Miss finishes handing out the card to each pupil and takes her place at the front of the room, one click of the keyboard and the whiteboard lights up with pictures of different family members. "Gratitude. I thought we could show some gratitude to the parents and carers in our lives. I thought it would be nice to create a little something for the mothers and fathers in your lives or anyone who looks after you." There's a glance in my direction on the words fathers. I'm sure of it. It feels like any second now, all the eyes in the room will turn and stare at me and Elliot.

The fatherless freaks.

That could be the name of a lame rock band or an alternative self-help group. I know we're not the only ones. Anusha lost her dad to bowel cancer last year and Sophie's mum died of a heart attack when she was young. "You can create a card for any important figure in your life. Anyone who supports you. It could be a friendly neighbour or teacher!" She smiles. "But we can use this opportunity to say thank you to that special role model in your life. If you fold your card—" She drones on about how we could create a collage or poem but I can't help thinking about the certain figure I've *never* really had in my life.

A dad.

No, I stand corrected. I *do* have a dad but he's currently serving time and there's not really a poem that fits a dad incarcerated in prison. What rhymes with violent abuser or rot in hell? Some start decorating their cards with words and colourful images, even Lewis writes the words MUM AND DAD in thick black marker. What a lovely activity to show me what I *don't* have. I wonder what it would be like to sit at a table with a dad who asks about my day and pats me on the shoulder before taking me out in the garden to kick a ball around.

"Josh?" Elliot leans across the gap between the two tables. "You okay?" I look over to his card where he has written TOM in purple swirly letters.

I don't even have a Tom.

I want a Tom.

I had a Steve.

I didn't want a Steve.

Everyone else with a normal family at home and our dad will probably be on next month's Crimewatch. If I want to get an image of *my* dad, I might as well Google Cruxby's Most Wanted. I rip the card in two, put my coat on and wait for the bell to release me from this hell. Miss looks over but doesn't respond, both Lewis and Elliot are now staring at me. It's been a week or so since The Josh Show was airing, maybe it's time to bring out the sequel. Eventually, Miss clearly can't help herself and walks over, sliding the two pieces of torn card into her hand. "Are you okay, Josh? You could write a card for your mum?" I nod and stare out of the window at a group of younger pupils picking up some litter, a new punishment brought in this term by Mr Owen. The bell rings. "I'm here if you want to chat." She faces the class. "Take them home and finish them there. Have a good day everyone and stay out of trouble!"

Students start funnelling out of the door. I lurk at the back, in no hurry to do Maths with Miss Foster. Lewis comes over. "You alright mate? Let's agree to disagree about all that homeless nonsense, eh?"

I shrug. "Whatever."

"Look, what's the deal with Freddie? He's been asking after you. Says he hasn't heard from you since that night at the park with the police. He's not really the kind of person you should ignore. Believe me, I know that." He looks to the ground. "Please, do what he asks or I'm worried you'll regret it." I try to walk past him, but he grabs my arm. "Are you going to do what he says?"

"Bring stuff into school?"

He nods and looks around him. "Yes."

"Then you can tell him ... no. It's not happening."

His shoulders sink. "This was your choice. Remember that. There's a party up at the reservoir next Saturday evening.

A kind of big blow out before the exams. A lot of the year group is going. I think you should come."

I look at the screen that Miss still has projected. There're images of different dads: old ones with grey moustaches, ones that look like dodgy car salesmen and ones with young children perched on their shoulders. I would take any one of them over the pathetic excuses I've had in my life. "Josh?" Lewis stares at me. "Did you hear me? You comin' to the res or not? Maybe you can explain to Freddie why you're avoiding him." Noticing my blank expression, he repeats himself again. "Clowbridge reservoir. Next Saturday. 8pm. Bring your own drink."

There's part of me that feels sorry for Lewis. Before Cruxby, he had me to hang about with at school and now he's either walking around school on his own or being Freddie's lapdog. In last week's English lesson when we had to partner up to discuss the theme of guilt in Macbeth, it was Lewis left on his own, sitting at the back.

"Josh?"

"Yeah, I'll think about it. Maybe we can hang out a bit but without Freddie?"

"Unfortunately, it doesn't work like that." He stares out of the classroom window. "I'll see you at the res."

I walk out of the room straight into Elliot who follows me down the corridor. "Oi!" he shouts. "Wait for me. What did Lewis want?"

"Not much. There's a party at the res. He says everyone's invited."

"Everyone?"

His face is hopeful, still Matchstick who wants to be accepted. "Yeah? Everyone. You don't want to come, do you? It's not really your sort of thing."

"I might!" And he skips off down the corridor swinging his briefcase. "Oh! Guess what?"

"What?" I shout.

"I got in the talent show!"

\

CHAPTER TWELVE

ELLIOT

I look at the clock. Six pm. Mum still isn't home. I know from the calendar on the kitchen wall that she had a counsellor session at 9:30am this morning but there's nothing else written on it. Stirring the pasta in the pan, I check my phone again but no messages. She promised me she would get in touch if she was going to be late. The front door opens and she bustles through, art folder in hand. Her cheeks flushed. "Hi, love." She kisses me on the cheek and drops her clutter on the kitchen table. "Something smells good!"

I keep stirring the pasta. "Where've you been?" I can't disguise the annoyance in my voice.

Tying her hair back with an elastic band off her wrist, she comes to smell the Bolognese sauce cooking in another pan. "I told you. A counselling session with Dr Jonas." She avoids looking at me.

"No. That was this morning. Where have you been since then?"

"Really? This again. I have to report back to you?"

"Can't blame me for worrying."

She falls into the kitchen chair and rubs her forehead.

"This isn't fair. I've done everything asked of me, medication, sat opposite a total stranger and talked about pretty awful stuff from my past, numerous doctor's appointments. You need to remember I'm the parent in this relationship, and *you* do not get to stand there with a face like a smacked arse if I don't tell you every move I make every day of my life!"

I turn the hob off and sit opposite her. "Yes, you do. Sorry but you do have to tell me where you will be and when. You do have to tell me what time you'll be back. This is not a face of a *smacked arse*; this is the face of someone who's worried about you for years and rightly so when I came home from school and found you lying unconscious on your bedroom floor. That worry doesn't stop 'cause you met a lovely man called Clint. If anything, I worry even more!" She leans back and folds her arms. "Don't get me wrong. I could cry at how far you've come, and I'm so proud of you it hurts but does it wipe out all the crap before? No! All the days I'd wonder if you would get out of bed that day? The days where we had nothing to eat in the house but mouldy cheese! The endless days trying to concentrate at school but constantly worrying if you're up, dressed, eaten ... alive? No! I'm still—"

"I'm not doing this." Mum's voice is flat. She stands up and waves her arms in the air. "I can't win. Damned if I do and damned if I don't. Fine. If that's what you want. Punish me forever—"

"It's not punishment!" I shout. "I love you and I worry about you. You—"

"Enough!" She points at me. "You can eat alone tonight." She storms out of the kitchen like a scalded teenager, and I throw the wooden spatula at the door behind her. It clatters onto the floor. "Oh! I got in the talent show! Thanks for asking!" The bedroom door slams shut. My phone vibrates on the counter. Felicity.

> Hi. What you up to?

I type quickly, still bubbling about Mum.

> Arguing with my mum. You?

> My parents are out. Want to rehearse for
> the show? I've got popcorn!

My heart beats faster and I sit back down, the anger at
Mum and the sheer panic of being asked to go to Felicity's
house. It's a lot to take. My fingers hover over the buttons. Go
to her house? Just me and her? What would I wear? What
would I say? I can't go in my school uniform but what's the
alternative? I don't have smart clothes like the other boys at
school. I don't own the latest football kit or have anything
with a brand name. Mum once bought me a pair of trainers
from the catalogue with Nicks written on the side, trying to
convince me they were Nike. My T-shirts are from the local
supermarket or worse still, Mum has started to find some *great
finds* from the local charity shop. My phone vibrates again.

> Don't worry if you're busy.

Busy? What would I be doing? Sending my mum to bed?
Reading *Gulliver's Travels* for the umpteenth time? Making
Spaghetti Bolognese for one?

> That would be great

Argh!

> Sounds good. Send me your address x

Should I put a kiss? Would a kiss be too much? Would she ask me not to come? Would she sit me down at school and tell me I've the wrong idea about our friendship and maybe it's best we don't see each other anymore? Or would a kiss be an easy way of showing her that I like her more than friends?

> Sounds good. Send me your address.

I delete the kiss and send it. The phone beeps soon after.

> Great. Will send directions.

My fingers feel funny. She hasn't put a kiss. We're friends. That's it. *Do not get over excited, Elliot.* It'll turn you into a floundering fool, but I'm going to Felicity Hooper's house. Argh! I am going to Felicity Hooper's house! Don't overthink this Elliot and don't use her full name ... that's weird.

There are at least five discarded outfits lying in a heap on my bedroom floor and I'm starting to sweat. I opt for a plain white T-shirt and jeans; it seems the safest option, but I can't control my hair. It has a life of its own: water, gel, spit, and I still lose the battle. I sneak a peep into Mum's room and she's asleep, curled up above the sheets, so I leave a note telling her where I am and head into our back garden. Mum and I have been working on it since last year. Marcus Tullius Cicero once said, 'If you have a garden and a library, you have everything you need.' A single yellow rose has appeared on the bush we planted last year, and the purple azalea's looking beautiful. Bunches of daffodils show off their bright petals, and I grab a handful before walking out onto my street, holding them loosely by my side so I don't look too odd. It's quiet on my avenue. Families inside their homes, sitting down for their dinner, discussing their days at school or work, not arguing over the strict curfew they've imposed on their parents or throwing kitchen utensils at the door. To get to the richer side of Mallowbank, you have to walk through the park. I avoid the skate ramp, where the older teenagers hang out in the evening, and keep to the narrow, cobbled path around the edge. The small stone wall is covered with a canvas of colourful graffiti.

Following the instructions on my phone from Felicity, I arrive at a wide street with huge, detached houses, all with their own large driveway and iron gates. Eventually I arrive at her house, behind the gates, is a long, winding drive leading up to an impressive white house. I thought houses like this only existed in American TV shows! Mental note never to invite Felicity to my house. Pressing the buzzer, Felicity's soft voice comes through the speaker. "Hi. I'll open the gates. Walk up to the front door." The iron gates slowly open and I feel like I'm crossing a threshold into a life I'll never be a part of.

What was I thinking?

The whole of my house could fit into their garage. Elliot Hart with his second-hand T-shirt and ill-fitting tattered trainers doesn't belong in a house like this. I look at the metal sign near her door, *The Gables*. Her house doesn't even have a number! It has its own name! The black front door opens, and Felicity appears, my worries subsiding for a moment. She looks stunning, wearing tight blue jeans and a black shirt. My mouth suddenly feels dry.

"Hi," I croak and give her the lame looking daffodils, instantly regretting this gesture, it was meant to be romantic not awkward.

She smiles. "My favourite. Thank you." I follow her into the entrance hall. This house is huge! The entrance hall alone is a room in itself, burgundy carpet, panelled white walls, ornate ceilings. A large vase of pink carnations stands proudly on a mahogany table in the centre.

"Your house is—"

"I know," she bats her hand. "I know. It's a bit silly really, especially when we were chatting about the homeless at tutor time today. We don't need all this room, only me, Mum, and Dad. But Dad does like *nice things*." She scrunches her nose up at these words and I feel an urge to grab her and kiss her.

I should've put a kiss on that text message.

Coward.

"Where are they?" I utter.

"Who?"

"Your parents?"

"Oh. At a work event for my dad. They have a lot of them. Not sure what they involve except dressing up in expensive clothes and falling through the door in the early hours of the morning, shouting at each other to be quiet so as not to wake me up." She rolls her eyes.

"So, it's just me and you?"

"Yep, and Fudge." She nods to the snoring golden Labrador by the entrance to the kitchen. "But he won't tell on me." She winks. "Shall we go upstairs and discuss our performances? I'm so proud of you for getting back on that stage. I knew you had it!"

My cheeks flush. "Thank you."

Before I've time to get my head around the fact that I'm in Felicity Hooper's house and going up to her room, we've grabbed a glass of orange juice, some popcorn and are walking up the stairs. The walls on the staircase are filled with framed photographs of the three of them, black and white ones, which have clearly been taken by a professional who tells them what to wear, where to stand and how to smile. There are no photographs of me and Mum in our house. Felicity's bedroom is the size of the whole bottom floor of my house, filled with white wooden furniture including a large dressing table with lights around the mirror.

My eyes widen. "Your bedroom's massive! Mine's so small compared to this. You even have a double bed!"

She laughs. "Well, I'll have to see your bedroom one day." She looks at me and raises an eyebrow. My stomach feels funny. "What's it like?"

"What?"

"Your bedroom! Let me guess." She scratches her chin. "Tidy? Organised? Decluttered?"

"Is that what you think of me? I'd be embarrassed if you saw my bedroom. There're still remnants of my space obsession."

"Space?"

"Yeah, I still am a little." I take a bow. "Presenting your resident nerd. I had an astronaut duvet and planets everywhere."

"Aww. Maybe I've got you wrong, Bieber. Maybe you're an Armstrong or Aldrin."

"I would be Collins. The one everyone forgot!"

"Stop that."

"What?"

"Putting yourself down like that. You always do it." She sits amongst her cushions. "Why space then?"

I perch myself at the end of her bed. "Tough one. I think growing up with my mum, it was difficult at times, and I think it was my way of escaping. A whole universe to escape to. I would lie on my bed and watch the planets rotating and convince myself that this can't be it. There's more to this world. I know it doesn't make sense, but it helped me." I keep my eyes fixed on the noticeboard on her wall.

She moves over and sits next to me, slips her fingers into mine and my heart races. "It makes perfect sense to me, see that poster up there of Katharine Hepburn?" A large black and white poster of a woman in a white dress, holding a cigarette is stuck to her wall. "I think she's the most talented actress that's ever lived, and when my dad's preaching to me for the *millionth* time that I need to get a good career and make him proud, I look at Katharine and tell myself to follow *my* dreams and not his."

Our hands are still entwined, and I look at her. "We're a pair of hopeless romantics, aren't we?" She slowly nods and I wish I could read this situation. There should be a book on these situations. I want to kiss her. Should I kiss her? What if she turns her head in disgust? What if she laughs at me? I quickly stand and walk over to her noticeboard, pinned with a sheet of all the various clubs Felicity attends, horse riding, drama, dance, violin. "You've a busy life."

She looks at the noticeboard and tenses. "Yeah. Not sure how anyone can ever succeed in life without attending every club Mallowbank has to offer. If it was up to me—"

"Why is it not up to you?" I interrupt.

She sits back amongst the pink cushions, pulls her knees up tight to her chest and grabs her Alan Bennett script. "Daddy Hooper has my whole life mapped out. The first time I might have control of my own life is when I'm eighty and planning my own funeral." She forces a smile.

"But what about Katharine? What would she say?"

"She would take a drag of her cigarette and say in her husky American tones *ignore him*, but I need Daddy Hooper to pay for the course at Cruxby, so somehow, I need to prove to him that's what I should be doing. That's why the talent show is so important. I need to be *that* good that he has no choice but to let me go. You're going to apply, aren't you?"

I mess with a piece of blu-tac on her desk. "I think so. Josh thinks I should."

Her face falls and she grabs her script. "Let's get practising."

I go and sit back on her bed. "What's up?"

She shrugs. "I don't really get it. I know." She holds her hands up. "You saw Josh in a whole new light when you scarpered off to Cruxby, but for me." She pulls at the fluff on one of her cushions. "For me, there's no new light, all I see is a mean bully who would go out of his way to make your life a living hell."

I rest my hand on her leg which makes my fingers tingle. "I know, but you have to trust me on this one. He's a good person who made a lot of mistakes. His homelife was difficult—"

"So was yours! I didn't see you go around punching people!"

I grab her hand again. "Let's not talk about Josh tonight, but I do like it when you get protective over me. You always have been. Whenever there was trouble, this cute face would appear hiding under your red hood."

She looks back at her cushion. "It wasn't a coincidence."

"What wasn't?"

"Me turning up."

"What do you mean?"

She shakes her head. "It's silly. I wanted to hang out with you but didn't know what to say so I would find opportunities to bump into you and see if you would notice me." She squeals and hides behind her cushion. "Enough of this! I'm getting embarrassed. Rehearsal time! Let's prove Daddy Hooper what I can do and let's get you that scholarship!"

I edge closer, my heart thumping. I want to tell her she's the nicest, prettiest, smartest girl I've ever met. I want to tell her that I notice her in school too. I notice how when a teacher asks a question, she mouths the answers to herself and her hand hovers above the table, wanting to answer but unsure whether she'll get it right. I want to tell her that when she smiles, all my worries about Mum vanish momentarily. I want to tell her that she might be the best thing to have ever happened to me, but instead, I chicken out and squeak. "There's a party at the reservoir next Saturday, do you want to come?"

CHAPTER THIRTEEN

JOSH

I run my fingers along the grooves of the wood that's still drying on my bedroom windowsill. Mum's key holder is nearly finished. "Can you take Coral to school?" Mum appears, brushing her teeth and I quickly stuff the piece of wood under my cover. "I'll drop Saff off at the nursery on the way to work." Toothpaste froths from her mouth. Rummaging through the heap of clothes in the washing basket on the landing, I try to find one school jumper for Coral that does not have a questionable stain on it, ranging from dried toothpaste to baked beans. Mum comes back from the bathroom, tying her hair up whilst Saff's attached to her left leg. "Is that okay?"

I scrape off the baked bean stain with my fingernail. "Is what okay?"

"To take Coral to school?" she repeats.

"Yes." I stand, holding the least grubby jumper I could find. "It's fine."

"Joshy smelly pants!" Coral charges out of her room and headbutts me in the stomach. "Want to see my new dance? I've been practising at school. My friend Ellie thinks she can do it the best, but she can't. Watch me." She throws her body around like she's been electrocuted whilst I catch two flailing limbs and put the jumper on her.

"Girls!" Mum starts packing her handbag. "There's cereal on the table. Breakfast together before school?"

"Yeah!" Coral charges downstairs, tripping herself up whilst Mum mouths *thank you*.

I pop two slices of bread into the toaster whilst the girls shove Cheerios into their mouths. Coral tells us a lengthy story about a girl called Poppy from her school who has red hair, five rabbits and three stick insects.

"Oh!" Mum jumps up from the table and heads to the door. "A letter came for you yesterday." She returns to the kitchen holding a slim brown envelope in her hand. I reach for the letter, open it up and read. "Well?" Mum leans over my shoulder.

I throw the letter on the counter and shrug my shoulders. "Nothin' important, merely confirming what we already knew. Your son's stupid and now it's written down on paper for everyone to see in black and white."

She snatches the letter off the counter and reads it, her face crumpling. "Oh love. Don't say that. This is a positive. It needs to be properly diagnosed but it looks like you have dyslexia. This is why you find some parts of school more difficult than others, and if we know the reason, we can all support you." She places the letter back down and goes to touch my face, but I turn away.

"Slap a badge on me!" I shout. "Get a card! Actually, get a big fat helium balloon, or a banner in the sky. Josh McBride's stupid, but we've given it a name. Let's celebrate! Let's pop the champagne!" I grab Coral's hands and pretend to dance.

She pulls away. "What you doing? You weirdo."

"Did you not hear what Mum said? We're celebrating!

Your brother has dyslexia and for some reason Mum thinks *it's a positive*."

Mum's face falls. "Stop it, Josh. Don't be like that. I just think after all this time, it's a good thing that the teachers have spotted you're struggling and now we know why. I should've spotted it sooner. It all makes sense now. I remember when you were younger and how difficult you found it to remember nursery rhymes and I thought it was normal until I had the girls and they picked it up much quicker. It's my fault too and the school should've—"

"You carry on thinking this is a good thing, Mum." I take the empty cereal bowls and throw them in the sink. "And I will stay in the real world and accept that I *will* fail my exams. At least my way I can't be disappointed."

She comes over and places her hand gently on mine. "I wish you could see *you* the way I do. I wouldn't be here, dressing for work, living in my own house, away from Steve if it wasn't for you." Her voice is quiet, so the girls don't hear. "You should be walking to school with your mates and talking about cars or girls."

"Mum!"

"Or boys!" She laughs. "My point being that you're knee high in your sister's dirty washing and about to escort her to school. So," she taps my head. "Your brain might work differently but your heart works perfectly fine and that's what's important to me." She places her hand on my chest and even the two shrimps have silenced to listen to her passionate speech.

I don't have the heart to knock her down after that Oscar winning performance, but I also don't think giving my stupidity a fancy name is anything to rejoice about. I butter my cold toast and kiss her on the cheek. "Right shrimp, get your bag, we need to go."

As we leave the house, I hear Mum shouting. "You need to

go to the Learning Support Department at lunch see—"
before the door slams shut.

————

I pretend to be reading the notice on the wall as I wait for my
meeting with Nina, but I can't help thinking there's a pink
neon arrow above me which reads stupid or special.

"Ha! McBride. Finally found a place to call home, have
you?" Lewis' voice booms down the small corridor. I spin to
see him and Freddie standing there, clearly truanting class. It's
weird how Lewis acts differently when Freddie's around.

Freddie stops, leans on the wall, folds his arms and stares at
me. "You've gone quiet on me after that night, McBride. I
asked for a favour." His voice is raspy. "I thought you would
be someone I could rely on."

"I've been busy."

"Busy making new friends here." Lewis nudges Freddie
and laughs.

Freddie remains silent, eyes fixed on me. "Some might say
you're avoiding me. I'm not good enough for you?"

"Yeah," Lewis copies. "Are we not good enough for you?
Now you have freak Matchstick and these guys." He points to
two boys sitting on the picnic bench outside with Miss Minns,
the teaching assistant.

"Lewis." I snap. "It was you who asked me to go the res.
You—"

"The res?" Freddie interrupts. "You going there?"

"Yes." I keep my eyes fixed on Freddie's, refusing to be the
first to look away, a trick I perfected with Steve. "Why?"

"No reason. I'll see you there."

"Josh McBride!" Nina's voice distracts us all, as she
appears in the doorway, cradling her mug of coffee and
smiling. "Come in."

"We'll see you later, McBride." Freddie announces before sloping off. "See you Saturday!"

I follow Nina into the room, hands in my pockets, as she gestures for me to take a seat. "Friends of yours?"

"No."

"So, you would've seen in the letter we sent home and I wanted to explain the concessions which will be provided from the school."

"Concessions?"

"Yes, things the school will put in place to support you. Your exams are in a few weeks, so we need to get this organised today." She takes a seat at her desk and rifles through a large stack of paper. "Here it is. Okay, we will try different coloured paper and see if any help. You'll be given 25% extra time in assessments, a laptop to use and if you want it, a small room to sit in for your upcoming exams in May."

"A small room? Like a cupboard! You want to put me in a cupboard?"

"No! Not a cupboard! A small classroom." She places the paper down. "Less distractions. You and a handful of others can do your exams in a small room if you want. It's your call." She takes a sip of her coffee.

I think back to the assessments I've taken in class, watching everyone writing and feeling like all eyes were on the thicko at the front. "Yes. I would like a small room. Thank you."

"Look Josh, most people think of dyslexia as trouble reading but like most things it's a spectrum that can go from mild to severe. It's a positive that we've identified your struggles, and we move on from there."

"That's what my mum said too."

"Is it? Well listen to us both." She insists. "Do you play FIFA on the computer?"

"Yeah."

"The way I see it, undiagnosed dyslexia is like playing FIFA but it's been set to a really high difficulty level and nobody has told you. All your friends and family keep telling you, repeatedly, that it's on an easy level, so why do you keep losing matches? Now we can look at getting an official diagnosis and with the right intervention, that mode is the same as everyone else. Does that make sense?"

I laugh. "Not really, Nina."

CHAPTER FOURTEEN

ELLIOT

Ruby picks up the empty cardboard box Glenn handed her when she stumbled in late to this evening's meeting. "I know! I'm late again but I only saw the message that we're meeting on Thursday thirty minutes ago."

"Glenn moved it, he has an interview for a university course tomorrow."

"Fair enough, now please enlighten me. Why am I holding a shoebox?"

"Well," I squirt some orange paint onto the saucer, "If you did arrive on time, you would know that Glenn wants us to create an identity box. We need to paint it with colours which reflect our feelings and then we're to bring in items that reflect *who we are as a person.*" I do my best to mimic Glenn's voice. "Something to do with how we can lose our identity as young carers. Buckle in for the excitement, we're creating our own superheroes next month!"

She takes off her leather jacket and rolls up the sleeves of her top reaching for the black paint. "I like to be predictable." She winks and slashes a thick black streak across the lid. "And how are we today, Elliot?" She stops and stares at me.

"Remember I know this face. I've drawn this wonderful face." She chuckles and starts spreading more thick black paint across her box. "I see new stress lines have appeared on that forehead of yours. What's up? Do share. I need a distraction from home." She bites the end of her paintbrush. My phone vibrates. It's Mum.

Love you. x

I switch it off and put it back in my pocket. "Let's see. I went to Felicity's house last week and before you ask, nothing happened! I'm not saying I didn't want anything to happen. There was this moment I thought it might but then I remembered I'm the awkward ginger haired kid and reality slammed me in the face. I fell out with my mum 'cause I know she's lying to me and the last time she kept things from me she ended up in hospital." I laugh. "But I'm doing fine!"

"Woah!" She squirts some black paint on my saucer. "You need to come across to the dark side!"

We both laugh. "I was also thinking about what you said. You know? About my eyes dancing when I speak about singing."

"I'm very wise."

"I went back and did the audition, and I got a place in the talent show."

"That's great!"

"If I get decent references and prove I'm good enough at the talent show, then I might get on the course."

"So, why the worry lines then?"

"I still struggle to sing in front of an audience, do you think that's important?"

She laughs. "A tiny, insignificant little detail."

More black paint is splattered on the box. "Can I come and watch you in the show?"

"The talent show?"

"No. The Great British Bake Off on telly. Yes! The talent show."

"Really? Why?"

"Because I get my kicks out of watching school talent shows. Because you're in it!"

"Me too." Frankie shouts from the other table. "I'd like to come and watch you if I can get out of the house."

"And me!" Katie looks up and smiles.

"Looks like we've got a night out!" Glenn smiles. "I'll organise the transportation. George?"

He looks up from under his cap and nods.

"Thank you." My voice breaks. "That's really nice of you all but-but you really don't have to."

"We want to, don't we?" Ruby looks to the others who all nod eagerly, except for George who's retreated back under his cap.

"Thank you. I'm sure having you there will make my nerves better. Or not!" I laugh and look at Ruby who's staring out of the community centre window. "Okay, spotlight off me for one second. How are things with you? Your mum?" There's a moment of silence when the reality of why we're standing in the community centre painting shoe boxes hits us. George is sitting by his unpainted shoebox, and now looking at his phone, sometimes I wonder why he comes to these sessions with no intention of joining in the activities but maybe it's just knowing you're not alone.

"Much the same," she mumbles, painting the final part of her box black. "She's out of it on morphine, lying in bed and everyone else is doing their best then secretly crying in private."

I put my brush down and grab hold of her hand. "I'm sorry, Ruby. You don't deserve this." She shrugs. "You don't have to cry in private y'know? This shoulder right here is especially good for leaning on, and it's especially good for tough, red-haired girls too."

"That shoulder right there?"

"Yep."

"You can tell all that from one shoulder?"

"It's been scientifically proven."

"Ten more minutes then it's circle time," Glenn shouts.

"When Glenn calls it *circle time*, I picture us all sitting, cross legged on a carpet listening to The Gruffalo." Ruby laughs and we both look at Katie who's helping Frankie paint a large yellow star on her box.

"It's a bit full on at times," Ruby sits down on the plastic chair, her voice softer. "Sometimes I want to have friends round and watch a film or go to a party like a normal teenager and not pick up prescriptions or watch my mum and dad become shadows of the people they used to be. We used to be a family. We used to go out for walks. I used to go shopping with my mum and eat chicken and coleslaw at Nandos. I miss it." She wipes her hands on some kitchen roll Glenn has provided. "It sucks, really."

"It does suck." I put a large orange streak down the middle of mine. Ruby raises an eyebrow and I point to my hair before taking a seat next to her. "I would eat chicken and coleslaw with you."

"You would?"

"Yes."

"That might be the sweetest thing you've said to me." She laughs.

"Look, there's a party up at Clowbridge reservoir on Saturday. Me and Felicity are going. You should come. Can your dad take the evening off work?"

"What? Be the gooseberry with you two? No, thank you. I'd rather administer pain relief to my mum than see you two drool over each other."

"It'll be fun! Please come. I've never been invited to something like this before, and I need your help to not act like a total dork around her."

"Nope. Not happening and anyway, I'm your friend, not a miracle worker!"

Glenn gathers us back as a group and we share our painted shoeboxes. Frankie thanks Katie for her help and explains the star's to remind her to dream. Glenn asks why I chose the colours for mine and he wouldn't let me have because I'm a ginger, weird kid, so we went with funny, smart, and unique.

Ruby picks at the black paint on her fingers and looks over at me. "I'll come."

"What?"

"I need to remember I'm a teenager and not a nurse. I'll come to the party. If my dad can get the evening off work. Can't have my smart, unique—"

"Funny."

"My smart, unique, funny friend making a fool of himself, can I?"

I hug her tight. "Thank you. Thank you. Thank you."

At the end of the session, I stay behind and help Glenn stack up the chairs. "I'm good," Glenn says. "You get yourself home."

"Actually, Glenn." I place a chair down and sit on it. "I wanted to ask a favour."

He pulls a chair up to the table. "Course. Fire away."

I grab my bag and pull out the crumpled application form for the drama college, placing it on the table. "I want to apply for this course, but I have to write a personal statement. I'm not very good at talking about myself."

"Have you asked your mum for help?"

"No. She knows about it, but I want to see if I get offered the scholarship before discussing it with her again."

"I'm happy to help, Elliot, but I imagine your mum would like to be involved in this, too. Talk to her."

"I will ... soon."

"Okay." He gets a pen from his pocket. "Let's have a look."

CHAPTER FIFTEEN

JOSH

Marshall stands at the front of the classroom clutching our MOCK exams like Saff holds her favourite PJ Masks book. "I know what you're going to ask. Do these exams count towards anything? Technically, no."

"What's the point then?" Lewis hollers from the back.

"The point, Mister Pretty. Thanks for asking." He starts to place a question paper on each desk. "So you can experience what sitting a real GCSE paper feels like and we will get to know your strengths and weaknesses. The next time you sit this paper it'll be the real exam and no second chances, therefore—"

"Luckily, I've no weaknesses, Sir." Lewis sits back, smiles and winks at Sir.

Marshall rolls his eyes. "Prove it then."

Lewis looks at me, narrowing his eyes. Mum gave another dramatic speech this morning about *doing my best* and *that's all you can do*. It's weird, ever since they've stamped a dyslexia label on me, it's like Mum and the teachers are relieved, like someone has waved a magic wand and having light green coloured paper and 25% extra time in exams will suddenly make me be able to write a full essay on Macbeth. However, I don't need a magic wand to tell me they are all going to be very disappointed ... again. Marshall, trying his best not to draw attention to the fact that my paper is a totally different colour to the rest, quickly places it in front of me. Highlighter Girl looks over.

I hate this.

I hate being stupid and I hate being different to everyone else. I hate sitting at the front of class with my special paper because my brain doesn't work properly. Well guess what everyone? Newsflash! Fancy paper and extra minutes aren't going to fix this problem.

"Right, class." Marshall returns to the front. "You've forty-five minutes for this essay but there are those pupils that are allowed extra time." Are you kidding me? Why don't you shine a bloody torch on my face Sir and let everybody have a good stare? "I'll put a timer on the board, and everyone will stop when it ends, those who are allowed extra time." My face heats up. "I'll put a new timer on." I go for my bag, hold the handle tight, inch off my chair and then remember what I promised Mum and sit back down. "Everyone turn over their papers and make a start. Good luck!"

Highlighter Girl starts scribbling straight away. Nina was right, the words are moving less on this green paper and it's easier to read but that still doesn't mean I know how, I look at the paper, how ... *the character of Lady Macbeth is presented in the play?* I watched a YouTube video on Lady Macbeth at home, after Sir's advice, and I can't remember what it said. Coral made me play an episode of Paw Patrol instead. Will Sir be interested in my discussion of Skye the dog and how she's good at rescuing other dogs in peril danger?

There's a spot!

Something about a spot on the video. A spot! A stupid, stupid spot. What am I going to write? Lady Macbeth had a spot and needs to get her skin cleared up? A quotation we discussed in class, unsex me here! Everyone sniggered when Sir read that part aloud. Lady Macbeth has a spot, and she wants to be … a man? This isn't going well. The timer's going down fast, and I can feel myself slowly giving up. Everyone, bar Lewis, is head down, busy scribbling away on their sheets of lined paper. I told Nina I didn't need the small room until my actual exams, but I want it now.

I don't want to be here.

"Oi!" Lewis hisses, throwing a scrunched-up piece of paper at my feet. I look over to Marshall who's hidden behind a stack of exercise books, pick it up and read it.

Final chance. Whatever Freddie asked—do it.

I throw the paper on the floor. Why would I do anything for him? It was Freddie and his friends who ran away and got me in trouble with the police. I push the table away from me. Highlighter Girl's pencil case tumbles off the desk with a clatter, pens and crayons spilling across the classroom floor. Everyone stops and stares. Another rerun of Josh *disrupting the learning of others*.

"Josh?" Marshall stands, urgency in his voice. I stand too, walk across the classroom to Lewis. There's fear in his eyes. I recognise the look. He jumps up and backs towards the window. The room's silent. Walking straight up to him, I put my face as close to his as I can. Marshall's behind me, shouting at me to sit down. Lewis's eyes flicker, avoiding looking directly at me.

"You need to leave me alone." My teeth are clenched. "I'm not scared by you or him."

"You should be, Josh."

"Why?"

"You need to do what he says or—"

"Or what?"

He looks at me. "I can't say."

"Sure you can. Big, hard Lewis Pretty. Spit it out. What will happen if I don't do what he asks?"

"Josh!" Marshall grabs my shoulder. The class is staring, and Elliot shakes his head.

"You're not worth it." I return to my seat and put my head on the table.

The bell rings and I lift my head up off the table and put my coat on. "Leave your papers on your desk and off you go. Not long now till the real thing!" He laughs. I grab my bag. "Josh?" Marshall looks my way. "Stay there, please."

I throw my bag on the floor, put my hood over my head and lean back in the chair. Everyone leaves until it's just me and him in the room. He collects the papers and places them on his desk before grabbing a chair and sitting across from me at my desk. "You didn't write much?"

Well observed, Sir!

"You have the extra time if you need it?" I shrug. "Did you revise?" He continues.

"Tried." I mutter. "But I don't get it. Can I go now?" I stand up.

"Josh. Don't give up. You can do this. I'll get some stuff together to help you."

"It won't do any good, Sir. I think we both know how this will end."

CHAPTER SIXTEEN
ELLIOT

I fall on my bed and burrow my face into the pile of clothes. A pile of supermarket bought shorts and T-shirts two sizes too small that Mum ordered from the catalogue five years ago.

Mum appears in the doorway, paintbrush in hand. "Need some help?"

"No! I don't need my Mum to dress me! I'm sixteen years old for crying out loud!" My voice is high pitched. "I'm actually trying to pick an outfit which will *not* look like my mum's dressed me." My phone vibrates and I find it under a blue T-shirt with Homer Simpson's face on. It's Felicity.

Be at yours in ten.

Ten minutes! Felicity Hooper's going to be at my house in ten minutes! I find a green and purple tie-dyed T-shirt I made with Tom, stuff my face into it and silently scream.

"Stop that." Mum laughs. I throw the T-shirt on the floor. "Why all the effort anyway? Where are you going again?"

"I told you! There's a group of us meeting at the reservoir. A final year celebration thing." She can't help but smile that her awkward son has developed something that qualifies as a social life.

"Don't look so pleased! You should be telling me to stay out of trouble and be back at a decent hour."

"Ha! Stay out of trouble and be back by ten o'clock." She places a hand on my shoulder. "Do be safe Elliot. There was an awful incident when I was young up at the reservoir. You still haven't answered my question. Why all this effort?" She raises an eyebrow.

My shoulders drop. "Felicity's going, and it's the first party I've ever been invited to, and my legs look like pale twigs and none of my clothes fit and she's going to be *here in ten*." I look at my watch which I got off Tom, the hands are rockets and there are faded images of the planets on the purple strap. Boys with a space watch do not have a chance with girls like Felicity Hooper. "No, I stand corrected, eight minutes." Mum walks over to my wardrobe, humming a tune to herself, and rifles through what's left hanging up and not discarded on my floor or bed. She looks out the window and then takes some faded blue jeans from the hanger before leaving the room. "Is that it?" I shout. "Is that all your help? Thank you for nothing!" She returns seconds later, still humming, scissors in one hand and starts cutting my jeans up. "Mum!" She continues humming and goes back to the wardrobe and finds a black T-shirt. "Voila! Wear these. Simple T-shirt and cut-off jeans. Your purple cardigan if it gets cold. This will be perfect and then use some of my mousse in the bathroom for that unruly hair. Don't worry, I'll stall Felicity." She kisses my cheek and leaves the room. "You're welcome by the way!"

Walking into the kitchen, Mum and Felicity are sitting across from each other, each cradling a cup of tea. Felicity's wearing blue denim shorts and a tight red T-shirt, her tanned legs stretched out in front of her. I look at her. "Hi."

She smiles. "Hi."

We stare at each other.

"Okay, you two best get going. Now be safe tonight. Home by ten, Elliot. No later. And no drinking or drugs or—"

"Mum!"

Felicity laughs. "Don't worry Miss H. I'll look after him."

My cheeks blush. "Let's go."

Felicity springs from her chair. "Thanks for the tea, Miss H." She leaves her mug by the sink and bounces out the front door. It's a warm evening, the air carries the smell of summer. It's the kind of weather which slows you down; there's no rush or urgency to these evenings. Neighbours stop to talk over fences and young children race down the street with melting 99s in their hands. My phone beeps. Ruby.

> Runnin late Mum havin a bad day.

I quickly reply.

> No worries. Sorry about your mum.

Slipping my phone into my back pocket, I walk side by side with Felicity, our hands are so close that my fingers are tingling. An invisible, electric energy. I want to grab her hand so badly that it's all I can think of as we walk through a ginnel between two houses and take the winding cobbled path up to the top of Tor Hill. We talk about my mum and Clint and how she doesn't want to disappoint her parents but wants some freedom. We stop midway to catch our breath and take in the view. From this point, you can see the two villages of Mallowbank and Farnham, the river Cad dividing the two. A small white army of windmills stand on the hill opposite and a huge electricity pylon looms over us.

"Me and my dad would bring Fudge for long walks up

here. Since he got promoted I come up here on my own." She shivers and I place my cardi around her shoulders. We carry on walking past a rusted, discarded caravan and Felicity tells me how she loved spending time with her dad, playing I-spy and throwing sticks for Fudge. She explains how he's not there as much since he's become more successful at work.

"I don't have many memories of being outside with Mum," I reply. "It's like I was as much a prisoner in our home as my mum was. If it wasn't for Tom taking me out on day trips, all my childhood memories would be fictional stories I read. My childhood memories would be developing magical powers like Matilda or travelling inside a peach with James. Those stories were great, but they're not real, and I would've preferred my own anecdotes, my *own* stories of climbing trees with friends or playing my *own* game of Pooh sticks." There's a fallen tree in front of us and I hold Felicity's hand to help her climb over.

She jumps over the tree. "My dad likes to pretend he cares where I am. He would kill me if he knew I was here. He thinks I'm revising for our science exam at your house."

"Really? Well, I'll ask you some questions on photosynthesis when we get to the top, if you want?"

"Oh! A bit of photosynthesis. Very romantic. Sounds like a great date!"

I stop and look at her. "Date? Is this a date?"

She smiles at me and walks ahead. I race to catch up with her. Eventually Clowbridge reservoir comes into view, a large expanse of water surrounded by a small dry-stone wall. In the daytime, it's a hit with dog walkers and runners. In the evening, students from St. Cuthbert's and Farnham High meet here. I often hear others talking about the reservoir parties at school, but I've never been invited to one. Following the noise of music and laughter, we find a large group of teenagers on the small hillside by the res, a fire has been lit and grey smoke spirals into the evening sky, smaller groups have splintered off, drinking beer, smoking, dancing, chatting, laughing and listening to music.

I don't fit.

I've never fit.

My shoulders tense and suddenly Felicity's fingers slip into mine. I look down at our entwined hands and then up at her, she smiles and my chest swells.

We fit.

I squeeze her hand tight and a huge, daft grin spreads across my face, there's not a chance in hell I can play this cool. I'm holding Felicity Hooper's hand. I need to stop using her full name! This might be the happiest moment of my life so far and the scariest. What do I do now? Will someone please write a damn book for this! They'd make a fortune! Stop grinning like a madman might be the first chapter. One of the smaller groups erupts and starts chanting.

Down it!

In one!

Do it! Do it! Do it!

Josh is standing in the middle of a group, drinking from a beer can. He finishes it and tips it over his head to prove it's empty. Freddie slaps him on the back and hands him another one. Once he's finished that, he hands him another. Lewis is looking on.

Felicity looks over as Josh takes a theatrical bow to his audience before stumbling and falling onto the grass. "I don't get it." Freddie picks him up and his adoring crowd starts chanting again. "And you *still* think he's a changed man?" I had to admit that it could get weary defending Josh especially when seeing him like this, but Felicity would never understand what we've been through. She wasn't in Cruxby.

"Elliot!" Ruby strides over, folds and places her hands on her thighs. "That hill ..." She gasps. "Isn't for me! Pretty sure I just hurled my dinner up into my mouth!" She stands up straight, places a hand on her hip and takes a deep breath before noticing I'm holding hands with Felicity, her eyes widen and mine do too, as if to reply *don't make this a big deal!*

She grins at Felicity. "Sorry. Hi! I'm Ruby. Nice to meet you. Elliot's told me—"

"Elliot!" Josh stumbles through the thick grass, a beer in his hand and an unopened one in his pocket. "You came!" He wraps his arms around me and hugs me tight, once released I check to see if all my ribs are all still intact. "Do you want to know somethin'?" He looks at Felicity who looks down at her feet and kicks the grass. "I—" he slurs, "Love thiz boy." He pats my chest and Felicity looks up, tilts her head, and watches him swaying on the spot. She remains silent which I'm grateful for. Josh takes another gulp of his beer. "I do! I love him! We're verrry different. He doesn't get brought home by the police for one. He's a good boy." He pats my chest again. "And he doesn't have green paper. No sirree. No green paper for Elliot Hart. He's the bright brother—"

"Maybe slow down, eh?" I nod to the can he's holding. Lewis and Freddie look in Josh's direction. "And stay clear from them two. We know what happened last time you hung out with Freddie."

His eyes are red and unfocused, and he slaps my chest again. "Don't worry. We're all friends now, making up over a few beers."

"They're not your friends."

"That's why I love 'im! Always caring about others. Did you know we're brothers and I couldn't—"

Ruby coughs loudly and Josh suddenly notices her, trying to compose himself for a second but swaying and spilling his beer. "Hi." She waves. "Let me introduce myself. I'm Ruby.

Elliot's friend." She holds out her hand and Josh shakes it, his eyes squinting to try and work out if he knows her.

"Who are you?" he asks, bluntly.

"Josh!" I look at Ruby, "Sorry about him. He's not usually like this."

"Ha!" Felicity snorts.

"Me? I'm Ruby Flanagan. Good friend of Elliot's. Why don't you pass me one of those beers and we leave these two alone for a bit? We can get some fresh air."

"Fresh air!" he slurs. "We don't need fresh air. We are surrounded by fresh 'ir!" He throws his arms in the air and drops his beer. Ruby puts her arm through his, winks at me and they walk away.

CHAPTER SEVENTEEN

JOSH

"Then I got brought home by the police and I'm trying to prove to my mum that I'm not Steve and they've given me green paper and I still don't get it. They can give me all the green paper in the world and I jus' will not get it. I'm simply following in dear Steve's footsteps. I try and I try, and I try but it's no use ..." I squint to focus on the red-haired girl standing in front of me. "There doesn't seem any point in tryin' anymore. I'm all tried out." My shoulders sag. I suddenly feel sad. I don't know where this girl appeared from, but she's a really, really good listener. I steady myself on the rock I'm perched upon, look out to the reservoir, smile at the memories of taking Coral for walks around here when Steve was in one of his *moods*. Coral would insist on wearing her pink sparkly wellies with the unicorns on, and splash in every single puddle, making the walk three times longer than it should've been. I didn't mind. Time *out* of the house was much better than time *in* the house. The noise of the party's fainter, and I realise I've no idea how I got over to this side of the reservoir. Did I swim? Where's my beer? Maybe she drank it. She's still standing there. Maybe she's an angel.

My angel.

An angel dressed in a black vest top, blue ripped dungarees, and black boots. "Can I ask-ask you something?" The ground's moving.

She turns and smiles. "Yes."

"It's a really, really, really important question."

"Go on."

"Are you ready?"

"Yes!"

"Did you drink my beer?"

She smiles. "No. I did not drink your beer."

"Okay. Can I ask you something else?"

"Please do. It looks like I'm a fountain of knowledge tonight."

"Are you an angel?"

She laughs. I like that sound. I want to make her laugh again. "Tonight, my friend. I might be yours." She turns and stares back over the valley. "This view's really pretty. I live in Farnham. I've never been up here."

I continue to pat the ground, searching for my beer. Where the hell is it? "So, angel. You're friends with Elliot?" She nods. "How did you meet? I don't recognise you. I think I would recognise you. You are very recogni-recogno-recognisable."

She keeps looking out over the hills. "The number of beers you've consumed tonight, I don't think you would recognise your own mum. I know Elliot from the young carer's meetings. I'm a young carer too."

"That's crap." I want to say something more profound, but I've nothing in my head. It's empty. "I'm not very good at the words. Elliot's good with the words. He would know what to say. He would use some big fancy words but not me. I'm the stupid brother with no words."

She faces me and puts her hands in her pockets.

"Personally, I think you're spot on with the words. It is crap. My mum's dying from cancer and before I came out tonight, I had to administer morphine and check her catheter so the exact word for this would be ... crap. You're perfect with the words. I take it you are Josh, the half-brother."

I nod. "He's a good one y'know?"

"Who?"

"Elliot. He's not like me. No sirree. I'm the bad twin. Well, we're not twins but if we were I would be the bad one. Defunct. Ouch!" I can't see the red-haired angel anymore, but I can see the purply orange sky and feel the grass underneath my back.

"Woah!" The angel laughs. "Get up!" She reaches her arm out to help me. "No. You get down here. Look, it's beautiful. We can try and look at the stars together. Bet you can't find the Big Dipper! I do this sometimes with my sisters in the back garden. On some nights, you can see the Big Dipper and Orion's Belt buckle."

"That sounds very romantic, Patrick Moore, but less stargazing and more water for you. Come on." I try to focus on her hand, but every time I try to grab it ... it moves. What a silly game she's playing! I start giggling like a little kid.

"Stop moving! Stop it!" Eventually, there's a tight grip around my wrist and she pulls me up but we both tumble on the grass and I'm looking at the stars again.

A cry!

A yelp!

She's hurt!

I crawl onto my knees. "Angel? Angel?" She lifts herself off the grass and holds her forehead. "What is it, angel? Angel? Are you hurt?"

"It's nothing. I hit my head on that damn rock there." As she stands, a line of blood trickles down her left cheek.

"You're hurt! Did I do that?"

"No. I fell! It's fine. Come on."

"I did it! The bad twin." My chest aches and I sit cross-legged on the grass and want to cry.

"You didn't do—"

"There you are! We've been looking for you everywhere!" Elliot and Felicity appear. "Ruby!" Elliot rushes over to the red-haired girl. "What happened?"

She pushes Elliot's hand away. "It's nothing. Can everyone please stop making a fuss?" Felicity buzzes around her like a fly whilst giving me that *look*. The look I get off Mum and Marshall. The look I have become so used to in my life. The infamous disappointed frown. The we-thought-better-of-you-Josh glare. I stand up, back away two steps, steady myself on a nearby tree to stop the world spinning.

Elliot turns. "Josh? What happened?"

"Elliot! Will you please listen to me? He didn't do anything! I fell!" Ruby interjects.

"I—"

"Josh, she's bleeding!" Felicity shouts. "What did you do? Elliot tried to convince me you were a good person, but I didn't believe it for one single second. Look at you! You're wasted."

"Listen to me!" Ruby shouts.

"I—"

"Josh?" Elliot looks at me for an answer. "What happened?"

"I–"

"What Josh?" Felicity's voice is cold. "What lame excuse are you going to make up now?"

I see it in Elliot's eyes.

I see it in Felicity's eyes.

It makes sense now. I ruin everything. I turn and run.

CHAPTER EIGHTEEN

ELLIOT

Ruby winces as Felicity finds a tissue in her short's pocket and dabs on the gash above her eye. "Shouldn't we follow him?" Ruby asks, looking towards the forest.

"Who? Josh? He can look after himself." Felicity states. "Probably off to get another drink. I'd avoid him if I was you. He's bad news." She finishes cleaning the cut and then scowls at me, pointing a finger. "I told you. Didn't I tell you? He's *not* changed. Once a bully, always a bully. One trip to Cruxby made you forget everything he put you through, but I remember. I was there! I was privileged to a front row seat to witness all the stuff he threw your way. Every. Single. Day."

Ruby raises both her hands. "Woah! Stop! Please. Both of you. Will you listen to me for one second? He didn't do this!" She touches her cut and flinches.

"Sit down, Ruby." I gesture to an old fallen tree trunk on the grass and we all take a seat. Felicity sits close to me, and I tentatively put my arm around her, she leans into my shoulder, putting her hand on my leg. Her hair smells of the vanilla buns you can buy from the school canteen. "What happened?"

Ruby tries to rearrange her hair to hide the cut, but her

fringe is too short. "Remind me to think twice next time you invite me out! Josh didn't do this. I tried to help him up off the floor and we fell. I hit my head on that rock over there. Here's me, thinking I was leaving the drama at home!"

"I'm sorry, Ruby. You didn't need this and he's not usually this ... *emotional*."

"Pah!" Felicity snorts.

"He's not! He's had a lot going on recently with struggles at school and still coming to terms with Steve and Gavin. I think I should try and find him. We were quick to judge him and one thing I've learnt this year is not to judge people." Felicity shakes her head. "Please, believe me. He's not a bad guy, trouble just has a habit of following him."

"Because he welcomes it with open arms!"

"I need to get him home before he hurts himself. You and Ruby go back to the party, and I'll have a look in the forest."

"I'm not letting you go in there on your own," Felicity replies. "Although you might scare monsters off with those white legs!"

"Oi!" I laugh. "I'll be fine. I'll see you back on the hill in ten minutes and—"

"You two go and find him," Ruby interrupts. "I'll take the path and meet you back at the hill."

"No. I'm not leaving you. You've had a bang to the head."

"I'll hit you on the head if you keep fussing." She smiles and winks. "You two go. Meet me back there in ten. I'll be fine."

"Are you sure?"

"Yes. Go!"

Holding Felicity's hand, we both clamber over the thorny undergrowth into the dark forest. "Trust me on this one Fee. Josh isn't a bad guy." The nettles scratch my bare legs.

"I trust *you*. I don't trust *him*." She stops and pulls me back. "And Fee? That's the first time you've called me that."

"Is it?"

"Yes." She smiles. "I like it."

It feels like the moment I should kiss her, but I've never kissed a girl before and I could be reading this all wrong. "Come on. We need to find him." We use the torch on our mobile phones to navigate ourselves through the darkness, shouting Josh's name repeatedly but there's no response. I move a low branch out of Felicity's way. "This isn't how I saw tonight going. God knows what Ruby's thinking!"

Felicity ducks down to avoid being decapitated by the branch and giggles. "I've no idea what you mean. Personally, I'm having a great time! Who doesn't want to be trekking through a dark forest trying to find your drunk brother with anger issues?"

I stop, hold both her hands in mine and turn her towards me. "I know he's made a lot of mistakes but there's a good heart lurking under all the … anger and alcohol."

She looks up to me. "You do know I witnessed all the horrible things he did to you. You didn't deserve any of that." We continue to look at each other and my heart races. Her arms are covered in goosebumps, and I rub them gently. She moves her arms around my waist and pulls me in, our bodies pressing up against each other. Tucking a strand of auburn hair behind her ear, I pull her even closer, stroke her cheek with the back of my hand. This is it. Don't ruin it, Elliot. My heart's beating fast.

"I could stare at you forever," I whisper. "Not stare at you in a stalker kind of way. That would be weird. I meant I could look at—"

She presses a finger to my mouth. "Now might be a time to stop talking, Bieber." We lean in towards each other, our lips inches apart.

"JOSH!" A terrifying scream tears through the trees. More screams. We freeze. The sound of terrified teenagers ricochets through the valley. We turn and run towards the reservoir. Keeping Felicity close, I race through the large conifers, jumping over rotten tree stumps, and holding her up when she stumbles on a large rock. The cries become louder, more panic stricken, more urgent. We arrive at the clearing, groups of people have moved towards the edge of the reservoir, the stone wall stopping them from falling in. Some are turning away, being comforted by others, some are on their phones shouting for help and waving frantically. Ruby's standing on the wall, flailing her arms. "Elliot! Elliot!" she hollers. "Over here! He's in the water. It's Josh! He's in the water!" I let go of Felicity's hand and race to meet her. "Look! Over there! It's him!" She points to a mass in the reservoir, which looks like a floating bin bag. I kick off my shoes and jump into the cold, dark water below.

My breath's ripped away and it feels like a thousand needles are jabbing into my skin. Floundering helplessly, I start to swallow mouthfuls of dirty water. My breaths are more ragged and urgent, and with each one I'm taking in more water. I'm disorientated, panicking.

It's too dark.

It's too cold.

What should I do? Go back? I can't do this. There's shouting from the edge of the water, but I can't see Josh. I turn around and around in the water, swimming in circles and kicking my legs as hard as I can. My breathing's too quick, too strained. I can't see him. Where is he?

"Elliot! There! He's over there!" Ruby and Felicity are jumping up and down, pointing to my right where I see the familiar black shape floating in the water like a lost buoy. Pushing my hands through the cold water, I try to get to him.

I must get to him.

I have to get to him.

I kick hard but my clothes are weighing me down. I swim

harder, push harder, kick harder, but I don't feel like I'm moving. I concentrate on each individual stroke instead of the impossible distance I must make to reach him. I get closer, he's face down in the water, bobbing up and down like a discarded sack of clothes. My legs are burning and refusing to move any more. Heavy weights dragging me to the bottom of the reservoir. I'm not moving now. My breathing's slowing down.

I'm tired.

Too tired.

I kick my legs slowly and reach Josh, rest my head on his back. *Josh, what have you done?* My eyes are heavy. This isn't how we go. This isn't our story. I think of Mum and Tom. This is *not* our ending. I grab his sodden T-shirt with both hands and scream whilst pulling him over. His pale face lights up under the moon's watch, hair plastered against his forehead, blue lips and eyes shut.

Motionless.

Dead.

I turn onto my back, drag his heavy weight onto my stomach and put my arms under his. Kick Elliot. Don't think of anything else and kick. Keep kicking. Kick and kick and kick again. My legs move slowly like forcing their way through thick treacle. "I've got you, Josh. I've got you. I'm in your corner. I've got you Josh. I've got you Josh. I'm in your corner." If I keep talking, I'm not drowning. If I can talk. I'm not dead. I think back to the police officer who came into school and showed us water safety videos. It said clearly, don't jump into open water.

Did you watch that video, Josh?

What party trick was this one?

Look at me ... I can kill myself.

Kick.

Kick.

Kick.

Kick.

Kick for every bad hand we've been dealt in our lives. Kick against the bullying, the name-calling, the teasing, the ignoring. Kick for every day Mum stayed in bed, for every evening I spent alone eating beans on toast. Kick for Gavin Turner, for hurting my mum. Kick for any other women he hurt. Kick for you, Josh. Kick for Steve. Kick for all the times he made you feel scared. Kick for all the times he hurt you. The shouts are getting louder. I'm getting closer. I recognise Ruby's voice and hear Felicity's panicked cries. Josh is too heavy for me to turn around and check I'm going in the right direction. All I can see is the dark sky and one solitary shining star.

A star.

I'm not in the water now but I'm lying in my bed, under my spaceman duvet, and Mum's having a bad day. I'm looking out of my bedroom window, and I'm staring at the first star that appears that night.

Am I still kicking?

My legs are on fire. Our bodies are sinking. I search for the star. There's a rhyme Tom taught me. I'm not moving anymore, and water's rising above our faces. I'm back in my bed. Tom is next to me.

What was that rhyme, Tom?

You know it, son.

I can't remember it. Teach it to me.

Yes, you can. Repeat after me, star bright, star light...

Star bright, star light ...

Keep going, son.

I can't.

Yes, you can. Keep going.

Star bright, star light. The first star I see tonight, I wish I may, I wish I might, have the wish I wish tonight.

Tom?

Tom?

Where are you, Tom?

Tom? I need you.

I let go of Josh and start to sink.

I'm here, son. I'm always here. Keep going.

My face comes out of the water, and I gulp the air, grab Josh and kick one last time with any strength left in me. A searing pain shoots up both my legs. Suddenly, an octopus of arms grabs my T-shirt, pulling and tugging. I'm heaved up and dragged over the wall, rolled onto the grass.

"I wish ..." I stutter. My body's shaking.

"Elliot." It's Felicity. She shakes me. "Elliot! Open your eyes! Elliot! Please! Open your eyes!"

"I wish ..."

My head rolls to the side and I open my eyes to see two men dressed in green. I'm wrapped in something shiny. Strong hands are on me. "You're going to be okay." A stranger's deep voice reassures me. Josh is on the grass, arms out wide like Jesus on the crucifix, not moving.

One of the men in green tilts his head back, shouts his name loudly. "Josh! Josh! Wake up, Josh!" I try to shout, try to tell him to wake up and explain this is not our ending but I've no voice. The man leans in and puts his face next to Josh's, they press hard on his chest.

Again, and again.

But he's not moving.

"I wish I may, I wish I might, have the wish I wish tonight."

CHAPTER NINETEEN

JOSH

"Josh? Can you hear me? It's Elliot."

Where am I?

"I'm glad you're sleeping because I wanted to say a few things and it might be best if your eyes are shut and you can't reply. I wanted to come here and say you're stupid. Yes. You heard me. It turns out you were right all along. You. Are. Stupid. Stupid. Stupid. Stupid. What were you thinking? Jumping into that reservoir! Some are saying they saw you jump. I know you were wasted, but really? Jumping into a cold reservoir? Utter death wish. You're a selfish, selfish, selfish individual and I'm so angry at you right now that I would hit you but you're still quite tough and I would probably lose even if you are passed out."

He's crying.

"Do you have any idea how important you are to me? There was a moment tonight, when I saw you in the water and I thought you were dead, and I thought I was going to lose you. That can't happen. My life since we found out we were brothers, well ... it's better. Yes, it's more dramatic! I'm sitting here in a hospital ward talking to my brother who almost died but it's ... better! Since our trip to Cruxby, I've been attending young carer meetings, making friends, Mum's leaving the house, and I might even have a chance with Felicity Hooper! This would not have happened if you didn't barge into my life and show me what I could be. You made me braver. You made me feel like I'm worth something. You made me feel safe."

More tears.

"And your mum and your sisters? You are their utter world. What would it do to them if anything happened to you? They see what I see! How dare you think so little of yourself? How dare you think so little of us. I hate you right now."

————

My eyes open to see a nurse pressing buttons on the machine beside my hospital bed, placing something tight around my left arm. My throat hurts and my head pounds. There's a slice of sunlight coming through one of the windows.

"Good morning, sunshine." She smiles and presses another button which makes the sleeve on my arm go tight, something tells me she's been here a while. "How are you feeling? I'm Holly, been on duty through the night. You gave us all a scare!" Cloudy images form in my head of a forest, shadows, a red-haired girl, water, coldness.

"What happened?" It's hard to speak. My throat feels like razor blades are stuck in it. There's a needle sticking in the top of my hand.

"You were found unconscious in Clowbridge reservoir and looking at your bloods ... slightly inebriated." The black thing on my arm loosens and she looks at the screen. "You seem okay now though. You'll hurt for a while and have the hangover from hell, but we're out of the woods and there should be no lasting damage. The doctor wants to keep you in for one more night in case you show any signs of secondary drowning."

"Secondary drowning? How did I ... first drown?"

She smiles. "That's the million dollar question the doctors and your mum want the answers to, but for now? You're alive and stable. Secondary drowning is very serious, but we will monitor you closely." She sticks a thermometer in my ear and waits for a beep.

"Is Elliot okay?"

"Elliot?"

"Ginger, tall, looks like a matchstick?"

"Ahh! Yes, he came in the other ambulance, but he's fine and was discharged in the early hours of the morning after a thorough check up."

"Heard you were here." Marshall's face appears around the green curtain of the hospital cubicle, and I suddenly feel very exposed in my hospital gown and tuck the bed sheets down. "Can I?" He looks at Holly and the empty chair by my bed.

"Feel free. I'm done here." She looks at her watch. "But don't be too long, this boy needs his rest. By the way, your mum's been sitting by your bedside most of the night. She's gone to get you some pyjamas and a toothbrush but told me to tell you if you wake up again, she won't be long." Holly takes the black sleeve off my arm, writes on the board clipped to the end of my bed and scuttles behind the curtain.

Marshall strides to the chair wearing a purple polo-neck T-shirt, jeans, and trainers, looking more like someone's dad than the grumpy Marshall I see at school. He sits next to my bed, resting his hand on mine. "Well, didn't you give everyone a fright?"

"Did I?"

"Oh yes! The whole of Mallowbank was woken up with sirens and flashing lights."

I mess with a loose thread on the bed sheet. "I'm sorry. Am I in trouble?"

"Trouble? Why? Because I'm here? Oh no!" He shakes his head and smiles. "Well, maybe with your mum. I'm here visiting my dad in the next ward and thought I would pop in on my favourite pupil and see how he is." There's a heavy weight pressing down on my chest, like a concrete slab's resting there.

"Your dad? Is he sick, Sir?"

Marshall shuffles in his chair. "Yeah, battling lung cancer and losing ... unfair fight if you ask me. He doesn't stand a chance."

"I'm sorry, Sir."

His shoulders drop. "That's very kind of you to say, Josh. It's tough to watch the man you look up to all your life looking so ... weak." His eyes glaze over but he shakes his head. "Anyway, let's focus on you. It sounds like you'll recover?"

"Yes, the nurse said I should be fine, but they're going to keep me in for one more night to watch for signs of secondary drowning, which I don't really understand because I'm not going in the water ever again."

He smiles. "It doesn't mean you drown in the reservoir again. Secondary drowning means there might be a build-up of water in your lungs, but they'll watch you closely. You're in the best place. Sometimes if someone has drowned or struggled in water, they can look like they are fine but then become very poorly a day or two after. You rest and let them look after you." He squeezes my hand. "What happened last night?"

"I honestly don't know how I got in the water, Sir. I don't remember much. I had a couple of drinks with Lewis and Freddie."

"Josh!"

"I know. I've messed up again." My head falls back onto the pillow.

"Okay, don't worry about that now. What's important is that you and Elliot are okay."

"Elliot is okay, isn't he?"

"Yes, he was in the water too but he's safe and fine." He looks at his watch. "You rest up. I best go and see how my dad's doing now, but can you promise me one thing?" I look at him and nod. "Come and see me once you're back at school. Everyone needs an extra helping hand occasionally, and I think it's about time you accept mine." He leaves me alone in the cubicle and I pick at a piece of dry skin on my lip and think back to last night. How did I end up in the water? Why was Elliot there?

Did I fall?

Was I pushed?

Did I jump?

"Was that Mr Marshall I just saw leaving the ward? What was *he* doing here?" Elliot strides in and takes a seat, like he's been here before. He's pale and dishevelled, reaching for a bite of toast leftover from the breakfast the nurse must have brought round. I look at him, try to piece together fragments of the night. I remember Elliot crying and calling me stupid. Elliot's friend, the girl with red hair. The angel. Blood.

"He's visiting his dad in the next ward." A wave of emotion floods over me. "What the hell happened, Elliot?" I gush. "How did I end up here? I don't remember. What did I do? Are you okay?" Tears fall down my cheeks and I wipe them away with the back of my hand.

"I'm fine, you big buffoon! I had an exciting trip in an ambulance and a few check-ups but now I'm discharged with a bunch of leaflets and Mum watching me very closely. I don't think she knows whether to hug me or hit me. Be warned though. Your mum?" He grimaces. "Your mum's *very* upset.

We managed to calm her down and the girls slept at mine. We've had poor Tom doing shuttle runs all night and I think he might be admitted next! It's going to kill him off! He's told me at least three times that he's not happy with the cheap coffee at the vending machine."

More tears fall down my cheeks. "I've messed up. Really bad this time. I'm so sorry."

"Josh?" Elliot pulls his chair closer to my bed, and it squeaks on the floor. "Can you tell me how you ended up in the water? You were pretty wasted but ... I need to know if you ... jumped," he whispers the last word.

"Jumped? No!" My head falls to the side. "Did I?" I remember drinking and I remember a girl with blood on her head. "Maybe? I don't think I did. I don't remember. Did I hurt that girl? Your friend?"

"No! It wasn't the best first impression you've ever given but she fell and hit her head on a rock. Successful night all round! But you didn't hurt her and anyway, Ruby can handle herself. She's the one who spotted you floating in the water."

"Ruby?"

"Yes, that's her name. Although she said you called her an angel!" He laughs. "And looking at you now compared to how you looked floating in that water, maybe she *is* your angel!"

More tears fall down my cheeks. "I wish I could remember what happened. How did I get out of the water? Did the paramedics go in? Was everyone there? Did everyone see?" Elliot sits back with a knowing smile on his face. "Did *you* get me out?" He nods. "Why would you do that? Did you jump in after me?"

"Well," He messes with the cuff on his sleeve. "*Jumped* might be pushing it a little. I would say a graceful bomb into the water would be a more apt description. And why? Because I care about you and don't want you to die!"

I wipe more tears off my cheeks. "I can't believe you saved my life with those twig-like arms!"

"Oi!"

We look at each other. "I don't deserve you."

"Maybe not but you're stuck with me."

The shrieking of two young girls pierces the quietness of the ward. Coral and Saff race into the cubicle and jump on my bed, simultaneously bouncing and firing off questions without waiting for the answer: *Are you sick? Are you going to die? What have you eaten? Why are you wearing that?* Coral jumps on my stomach and Elliot lifts her off. "Mummy's very angry, but we stayed at 'Liot's house and had cookies after midnight and watched cartoons. 'Liot's mummy let us sleep in her bed with her and we read books and told stories and—" Mum walks in, guiding Saff off the bed before Elliot kindly offers to show them what culinary delights they can find in the vending machine.

She dumps a plastic carrier bag on the chair and sits on the edge of my bed, her face pale and blotchy, eyes fixed on the floor. "It's good to see you're awake. I've been here all night, but you weren't making much sense, mumbling about an angel. I've spoken with the doctor this morning and they are keeping you in for observation. They've mentioned something called secondary drowning and—" I grab her hand and squeeze tight, but she shakes me off and folds her arms, still refusing to look at me. "I've brought you some clean pyjamas and visiting hours end soon so—"

"Mum!" My voice is loud, she stops talking and eventually looks my way, her eyes filling with tears which she swiftly wipes away. "Mum. I'm so, so sorry." I start to cry again.

Her face crumples and she drops her head into her hands. "I can't do this. I can't do this anymore. I can't speak about this right now. I honestly don't know what to say to you. I could've lost you last night. They had to do CPR, Josh! Do you know what that means? You technically died. Your heart stopped. If they didn't get there in time and if Elliot hadn't pulled you out of the water." She slaps my leg. "What the hell were you thinking? Jumping into a reservoir. I can't lose you."

"I don't know. I'm sorry." Tears fall down my cheeks. "I don't know what happened. I know I've promised this a thousand times and there's no reason for you to believe me this time, but I'll keep trying to be better. Do better. I'll keep trying. I don't deserve any of you."

She leans in and hugs me tight, her face buried in my neck. "Yes, you do. You deserve all of it. We love you," she whispers. "Why can't you see that?" The girls bound back through the gap in the curtain and hurl themselves on my bed. Elliot walks over and squeezes my shoulder before leaning in for some more cold toast. Tom arrives shortly after, walking stick in hand, he smiles and his whole face creases. "You daft idiot!" He laughs, shakes his head and places a half-eaten punnet of grapes on the cabinet. "I do apologise for the gift, but I've been a taxi service for most of the night, and I didn't have time to get you anything, so I fetched these from my fridge."

"Thanks, Tom."

Holly returns and asks everyone to leave so I can get some rest. Once I'm hugged tightly by all of them and Mum's eventually persuaded to release me, they leave, and Holly plumps up my pillow. "You're one lucky boy."

"I know." My eyes are heavy. "They tell me I'm lucky to be alive."

Familiar voices can be heard from the corridor, and she shakes her head. "That's not what I meant."

CHAPTER TWENTY

ELLIOT

After dropping Josh's mum and the girls off, me and Tom pull up outside his house and I follow him in, putting my arm under his and leading him to the living room. He's more unsteady on his feet than I remember, and I don't think ferrying the McBrides around Mallowbank all night's helped. As he falls into his beloved armchair, he breathes a sigh of relief. "That's better. What a night! And no more crazy heroic stunts from you. This old man can't take it and you're very precious to me."

"Tom?"

"Yes."

"Last night when I was in the water with Josh, there was a moment when I thought I might not make it, and I heard your voice. I know that sounds silly, but I did! You told me to keep going."

He adjusts his position in the chair and rests a cushion on his lap, takes his glasses off and massages the bridge of his nose. "It's not worth thinking about. The what ifs and what could have happened. Why don't you put the kettle on, son? I think we could both have a cup of tea."

I walk over and kiss him on the cheek. His skin's paper thin and cold. "You're very precious to me, too."

In the kitchen, dirty cups are stacked up by the sink and what looks like yesterday's porridge is crusting in a bowl on the counter. Tom is usually so meticulously clean. I get a cloth and wipe down the counters, wash the dirty dishes in the sink before making us both a cup of tea. "I can't get my head around last night, Tom. It was crazy. Just before Josh went in the water, Felicity and I were in the forest and well, I might have misread it, but I honestly don't think I did ... I think we were about to kiss. I think she likes me!" I can't stop smiling. "And when I was in that water, I thought I wouldn't make it and I don't want to die without kissing Felicity. Anyway, I'll come round tomorrow and vacuum the—" I stop in the doorway, two mugs in each hand and smile, gentle snoring rises from the chair in the corner. Taking the throw off the settee, I place it over him and kiss him on the forehead.

Back home, Mum's sitting in the living room, curled up under a purple blanket, half watching the breakfast news. More paintings are resting by the fireplace. She's nearly finished the painting of the lake. The sun's setting in this one, oranges and reds fill the sky, and there's an empty wooden boat moored up. A large swan's in the foreground, looking graceful but I imagine its feet are working hard underneath. There's another painting of a seafront with angry, grey skies and huge, crashing waves. This one's more like her old style, lots of small people along the seafront, some sitting on benches, another appears to be busking and there's a couple holding hands but if you look closely, you will see that no one's looking at each other. There are arcades in the background and a broken neon light with the pink letter R falling off. Felt tips are scattered across the living room floor, and I can see the girls have started making get well soon cards for Josh. Mum lifts the blanket and nods for me to join her.

Suddenly, my body shouts and screams how tired it is. Each limb feels like lead, and I feel sick. I join Mum under the blanket and stare at the screen, half watching an exuberant weather presenter inform us the sun will be shining all day. Mum doesn't look at me. "You understand that we need to chat about last night, don't you?" She says matter of factly. My head falls onto her shoulder and she pats my cheek. "But not today. The doctor says you need to rest." My eyes are heavy. "Can you tell me one thing though?" I nod. "How did it go with Felicity? You know, before you decided to become Mallowbank's superhero and jump into a freezing cold reservoir."

I struggle to keep my eyes open, and stretch my legs out along the settee, then take myself back to standing in the forest with Felicity, our hands entwined, our bodies pushed together. "It went well, Mum. I've a feeling everything's going to be okay."

"That's nice to hear. A superhero and a Romeo tonight then?"

"I'm going to go for it, y'know?"

"Go for what, sweetheart?"

"Everything. I could've died tonight. I'm going to go for the scholarship, the talent show. I'm going to go for Felicity. I'm going to go for all of it."

She strokes my hair. "Okay superhero. Now get some sleep."

"Can you promise me one thing, Mum?"

"To the boy who put me through hell tonight? Yes, of course, anything."

"The talent show's next week. If I get you and Tom tickets, will you come and watch me?"

And before I succumb to a deep sleep, I hear her say, "I wouldn't miss it for the world."

CHAPTER TWENTY-ONE

JOSH

Marshall looks up from his pile of exercise books and smiles. "Josh!" He quickly stands up, meets me at the door of his classroom and shakes my hand. "Good morning." He looks at his watch. "This is early. School hasn't even started yet, but it's good to have you back. We've missed you in class."

"Really?"

"Yes, it's been a week! What am I meant to do with my time when I have no fights to break up or pupils storming out of my room?" He smiles. "How are things? How are you feeling?" He motions for me to take a seat by one of the desks and turns a chair around to sit opposite me.

"Okay. Well, I'm grounded till I'm eighty, but I feel fine. The doctors are happy I'm fully recovered but I'm not sure I've recovered from all the mum lectures though."

"Well ... be prepared. The lectures are carrying on at school. We're taking it very seriously. Mr Owen has some assemblies planned for next week about keeping safe around open water. It can be so dangerous. When I first moved to Mallowbank a teenager got into trouble up at the reservoir one summer. I remember it was a really hot, sunny day and he was up there with his brother and friends. Word got through that they had been in a terrible accident and there were so many police cars that afternoon. You were very lucky Josh, but we need to stress to you *and* all the pupils that sometimes the outcome can be a lot different. This boy was really fit, and strong but open water is so dangerous, and this should be common knowledge."

"I know. I know. I really do. My mum told me that story too."

"The shock of the cold water, you could've been the next teenager to lose their life up there." He tilts his head and looks at me. "Have you remembered how you ended up in the water yet? Mr Owen was worried you ... jumped. Mrs Spencer wants to book an appointment with you just to chat about how you're feeling."

"I don't think I jumped but I still don't remember anything." I hang my head and mess with the cuff of my school jumper. "I'm sorry about everything. I actually wanted to pop by and say thank you for the gifts you dropped off at my house. I'm also sorry for letting Lewis get to me in your lesson."

"We need to help you. I know Lewis knows how to get a response from you, but you need to control those feelings—"

"I know. I let things build up until I ... explode."

He leans back in his chair, crosses his legs, and folds his arms. "What kind of things?"

"Lots. The dyslexia for one. It felt like once I got the label everyone was happy and that was it, a magic wand had been waved and solved everything, but for me? Nothing changed. I still struggle and I still feel stupid."

"Stop that."

"What?"

"Calling yourself stupid. If you think you are stupid, then it's likely others will too. You're not stupid, Josh." I stare out of the window as the school yard fills with pupils. "Okay, if we're playing the sorry game, then it's my turn to apologise to *you*."

"What do you have to be sorry for, Sir?"

"I'm sorry for not spotting the dyslexia earlier." He leans forward and nods his head. "I should have. We ... as a school should have."

"It's not like I made it easy for you, prowling around the school with a big, massive chip on my shoulder. I did try in your lessons, but it turns out I have the attention span of a three-year-old on his tenth pack of Haribo. I was listening! It might not have been very interesting what you were saying but I was listening!"

He laughs. "That's good to know!"

"The gifts you dropped off at my house. I was annoyed at first that you wanted me to work when I was meant to be off sick, but I managed to listen to the audiobook of An Inspector Calls without my sisters interrupting me and I read the whole of Macbeth, turns out the graphic version is a little bit more interesting. Once I realised it was really about murders and ghosts and witches, it wasn't as boring as you make it sound in class."

"Thanks again!" He laughs.

"I didn't mean that, I meant—"

"I know. I did try to tell you on many occasions. Go on then, what did you like most about it?" I recount my favourite parts of the play and how shocking it was that someone could turn so evil because of something a bunch of witches say. He explains it's not as simple as that, and people can struggle with demons no one else can see.

"I agree, you could go through life blaming everyone else but eventually if they're your actions, the responsibility has to lie with you doesn't it, Sir?"

"Are we still talking about Macbeth, Josh?" He smiles. "What other things are on your mind?"

I think of Steve. I think of Mum's conversation to Vee on the phone and getting sent home by a police officer. "Lots. Lots of scorpions in my head, Sir!" He smiles at my reference to the play. "Sir, how's your dad doing?"

He looks out of the window. "He's not doing very well actually. They think it's a matter of days now, not weeks."

We sit in silence and look at the other students congregating on the yard. "Can I ask you something, Sir?"

"Yes."

"Why are you here if he only has days left? Don't you think you should be with him?"

He doesn't look at me. "Maybe. It helps though, coming into work. It's probably a distraction."

"Even though I give you hell?"

He smiles. "You describe it as *giving hell*, I describe it as a teenage boy struggling. You were struggling, Josh. You *are* struggling. That shows in different ways. With you? It tends to come out in a lot of frustration and anger."

"Do you know about my biological dad and step dad, Sir? Gavin Turner and Steve?"

"Yes, I read it in your file."

"I worry I'm like them. My anger and violence. What if no matter what I do, I end up like them?"

"You've just been talking about Macbeth, right? Responsibility. They had choices. All the way through they had choices. You do too. All the time. You chose to come and see me today. You chose to apologise. You chose to listen to the audiobook and read the play instead of throwing them in the bin! You're not a bad person, Josh. I've spoken to Mrs Stephens, and she's informed me what home life is like for you and how you care for your sisters. You seem like a pretty decent person to me who sometimes makes wrong choices, and we're all guilty of making wrong choices. That does not make us a bad person, if anything it simply makes us human. If you carry on making the right choices, it's impossible to end up like them. Try to forget about those people from your past and look at who you are right now and all the people that care about you." He walks to his desk. "Okay, one more text, A Christmas Carol by Charles Dickens. Graphic form again?" He hands me a book from his desk drawer with a picture of an old man in his nightgown on the front.

"Yes, please. Thank you. One more thing?" I bend the book, feeling uncomfortable. "Mrs Stephens has helped me fill in an application form for Farnham College. I need to put two references down. I'm going to ask Mr Hogg, but I was wondering if I could put your name down too? I know I've not been the easiest student—"

"I'd be honoured," he interrupts. The bell rings for registration and we both stand from our chairs. "I've created you a pack too—a framework for essays, some helpful websites, example essays. I'll give it to you in class."

"Thanks Sir." I shake his hand and turn before leaving the room. "Can I say something? I don't mean to step over the mark or anything."

"Go on."

"Go and be with your dad."

CHAPTER TWENTY-TWO

ELLIOT

Back stage of the drama studio is a hive of nerves and excitement. Mr Kay's in the middle, arms flapping wildly like he's trying to conduct a drunk orchestra. The year seven girls are in the corner rehearsing their Pussycat Dolls dance routine, screaming loudly and dramatically throwing their heads in their hands when one of them forgets a move. Scarlet Fisher from year nine is practising her magician tricks, pulling multicoloured handkerchiefs out of her sleeve and shuffling a pack of cards whilst Amita is taking refuge in a quieter corner, eyes closed, playing her cello. "Twenty minutes till showtime!" Mr Kay announces. The room bubbles over with squeals and clapping, mostly from the overexcited dance ensemble. I search for my own sanctuary and find a plastic chair near the coat rack. In less than thirty minutes, sandwiched between Scarlet and Kevin the comedian, I'll be waiting to go on stage and sing my own song whilst playing the guitar. In less than twenty nine minutes, it is likely I'll be throwing up in the toilet.

"George Washington, John Adams, Thomas Jefferson." A hand rests softly on my shoulder, Felicity's looking down at me and smiling. "Stop that. You don't need to do that thing you do with the lists anymore."

I force a smile and wish I had her optimism. "Tell me again, why am I putting myself through this? I knew we had a reason but right now, I can't for the life of me think what that would be."

"Because," she kneels on the floor in front of me and grabs both my hands. "It's about time people see what I see." She makes everything seem okay for a moment. We stare at each other, and the surrounding chaos becomes quieter. "You still haven't told me what you are singing yet. Why the big secret?"

"You'll find out soon enough. If my jelly legs let me get off this chair." She giggles and stands up. "What about you?" I ask. "How are you feeling? I see Sir has put you after me. Probably to cheer the crowd up after they've witnessed my car crash performance." She giggles again and I use all my energy to telepathically tell her to kiss me, right now, right on the lips.

Kiss me.

Kiss me.

Kiss me.

I wish I had Scarlet Fisher's magical powers.

Ruby cyclones into the room. "We're not worthy! We're not worthy!" She storms through the gaggle of nervous pupils and pretends to bow down to Felicity and I. Josh follows closely behind, avoiding Felicity's steely gaze. "Look who I found skulking outside, too nervous to come in." She gestures to Josh. "Didn't recognise him without the beer stench and eyes doing this." She points her fingers out of her eyes and wiggles them. Josh stays quiet, smiling, allowing Ruby to take centre stage. "We thought we would quickly sneak in and wish you both good–no–no, what is it? Break a leg! That's what they say isn't it? We've managed to reserve front row seats and saved two for your Mum and Tom too. I've seen the whole gang! Glenn! George! Katie! Frankie! They're all here to support you."

"Really?" My chest aches, especially as it is more difficult to get out of the house when you're a young carer. We don't have the same luxury as others. I'm worried about Mum. She's doing much better, but she hasn't been in a place as packed as this for a long time. A familiar knot tightens in my stomach. "Are they here yet, Josh? My mum and Tom?"

"Haven't seen them yet but then again, we've been too busy chatting outside." He smiles at Ruby.

"Ten minutes!" Mr Kay roars and a whole rope of knots tighten in my stomach. Ruby and Josh make a rushed exit whilst Felicity hunts for a mirror to check her makeup. I know she wants to prove something to her parents tonight, prove the drama course is her dream, not Science at Farnham college. There's so much chatter, laughter, music that I crave some peace, quietness, and stillness.

Clarity.

I need to keep my nerves under control. I don't want them to win again. This is my only chance to get that scholarship, and the tutor of the course will be sitting in the audience right now. I need to show them what I can do. I deserve this as much as anyone. Then it's time. Mr Kay asks for silence and leaves to greet the audience, ordering us to take a seat in order of appearance, wide eyed faces whispering *good lucks* and giving thumbs up. I take a seat in the middle of Scarlet and Felicity. Time passes and as each act leaves to have their moment in the spotlight, I hear rapturous applause. Felicity looks at me, puts her thumbs up and gives me a wide smile.

"Okay, Elliot. You're up now. This is your time. The tutor from the college is here so show him what you showed me. You've got this." Mr Kay's looming over me, he gives me a reassuring nod and then passes me a guitar, moving the red velvet curtain for me to go through. Lots of people are squeezed into the drama studio, line upon line of families and friends eager to see their precious loved ones perform on stage. The room falls silent as I shuffle across the polished, wooden stage floor, the squeak of my shoes echoing around the theatre. I stand at the microphone and suddenly a bright light shines in my face. I shield my eyes. My heart rattles against my throat. Putting the guitar strap over my shoulder, I look to the front row, Josh and Ruby are sitting there, leant forward, mouths slightly open.

Two empty seats next to them.

Mum and Tom aren't here.

I look at the vacant chairs and Josh shrugs his shoulders. Mr Kay appears at the side of the stage, looking nervous. "Come on," he mouths. Hushed whispers ripple across the audience. Placing my hands in the correct position on the guitar, I sing the first line, "Standing in the corridor with your red coat and the freckles on your nose." My voice sounds good. Glenn and the gang are sitting a few rows back. Frankie's smiling and George has his cap off, giving me the thumbs up. I'm playing the right notes. The relief from the audience is tangible, and I carry on singing, but images of Mum collapsed on the bedroom floor flash in my mind. The spit in her mouth.

Don't do this Elliot.

Don't let your mind win.

This is your only chance. I carry on singing, "You make me lost for words."

But she promised.

Where is she?

I've fallen silent. The frustrated whispers of the audience become louder, the scraping of chairs. I'm making them uncomfortable. "Get on with it!" a voice shouts from the back. Josh barks something in return and then looks at me and nods encouragingly. The scholarship. I need to get through this and deal with Mum later. They might be late, but Tom is always so punctual. He's never late. I start to play again but get the chord wrong. That familiar feeling of dread is sitting in the pit of my stomach, and I know something's wrong.

I wouldn't miss it for the world.

I let go of the guitar and it hangs loosely round my shoulders. There's Josh, Ruby, and Glenn, and there's two empty chairs. "I'm sorry." My voice is loud down the microphone and there's groans from the audience. "I can't do this." I take the guitar off my shoulders and pass it to a startled Mr Kay as I race off the stage.

"Elliot!" Felicity stands up and looks at me panicked. "What are you doing? This is your only chance. Do not leave now!"

"It's Mum. There's something wrong. I know it. I have to go."

"I'll come."

"Felicity," Mr Kay interrupts. "You're up." He nods to the stage, a sense of urgency in his voice.

She looks to me and then to Mr Kay before turning her back and walking onto the stage. I open the door and race down the long corridor and out of the school building. As I run across the filled car park, it begins to rain. The streetlights cast a hazy glow through the fog, the sky's turned purple and the trees sway in the wind. A loud rumble of thunder as the rain comes down harder forming huge puddles on the pavement. I race through the terraced streets, my chest pounding, my breath rasping. I'm back in that familiar place, praying that Mum's okay, forcing myself to picture her in the living room, her painting out, imagining her apologising profusely because she lost track of time. I picture her healthy and happy. I'm picturing it so hard to make it be true, but I know this feeling too well, something's wrong.

"Elliot!" Josh is behind me, shouting at me to stop, slow down, but I keep running and turn left onto Ivygreen Road.

Blue lights from the ambulance light up the street.

I bend double, a sharp pain in my stomach and support myself on a neighbour's wall. A strong arm grabs me around my waist, lifts me up. "I've got you." Josh half carries, and half supports me as we edge closer to the small crowd that's gathered outside my house, and I see the black body bag being lifted by two paramedics into the back of the waiting ambulance.

It's Mum.

She's dead.

CHAPTER TWENTY-THREE

JOSH

Ruby stands next to me in Elliot's kitchen. I look out of the window onto his back garden and the daffodils. The rain's stopped. She reaches for my hand. "How did he—"

"Heart attack. His mum went round to get a lift and there was no answer. She got in with her spare key and found him lying on the kitchen floor. Gone. Poor Vee. It must've been so scary." Tears escape down my cheeks, and I snatch my hand away from hers and turn away.

"Josh."

"Leave it. Please."

"Josh." She grabs my shoulders, spins me back around and wraps her arms around my waist. My heart races. Images of the black body bag. I step back, wipe my face with the back of my sleeve and grab the kettle. "Josh. You're allowed to be sad. You cared about him too."

"It's silly." I lean for the tap. "I'm being silly. It's them two in the living room who need looking after, not me. Ignore me."

She grabs my arm. "Josh. Stop. Please."

I turn towards her, our faces so close I can feel her breath on my skin. Suddenly, my hand grabs the back of her head, pulls her closer and I kiss her softly on the lips. I stop, breathless, my hand still holding the back of her neck. She's looped her fingers around my belt and pulls me closer, our lips still touching. I back away. *What am I doing?* Our eyes remain fixed on each other and I'm breathing hard. My cheeks are still wet from tears.

"Oh God!" I let go of her and step away from the kitchen counter. "I'm sorry. I didn't mean to ..." She reaches for me, but I take another step back. "I'm so sorry. I shouldn't have done that."

"Josh," she whispers. "Stop apologising."

"I'm so—" She grabs my T-shirt, pulls me towards her and kisses me on the lips, soft and gentle. We remain there, eyes closed, lips touching. Eventually, I pull away and she smiles, wiping my cheeks with the cuff of her sleeve. I step back and stare at her. "Not now. Not like this. Not that I don't want to." I place my hands softly on her cheeks and kiss her on the forehead. "But this is not the right time."

She places her hands over mine and nods. "I know."

We make two cups of tea for Vee and Elliot and head back into the living room. A collection of paintings lean by the fireplace, one of her and Elliot by the cenotaph in the square. Vee's sitting on the settee, wearing a red dress, a tattered tissue in her hand and staring at a blank television screen. I let go of Ruby's hand and step away from her. Elliot's standing by the front window, looking out to where the ambulance and paramedics were. Ruby passes Vee a mug and sits next to her, placing a hand gently on her leg. I walk over to Elliot, offer him a cup but he shakes his head, his arms folded tight. We remain in silence for a long time. Ruby and I stare at the floor, Vee at the blank screen and Elliot out onto the street. I try to think of something to say but everything I think of seems inappropriate and unhelpful. The tick tock of the clock on the mantelpiece is the only sound to break the heavy silence.

"Did he have any family?" Ruby's voice is gentle and cautious, testing the moment, wanting to respect the silence in the room and the enormity of the situation. Vee shakes her head, tears falling down her cheeks. "No." she sniffs. "Only Edna. His wife. But she passed soon after Elliot was born. He can be with her—"

"No!" Elliot's voice is loud and startles the room. "No!" He turns and runs out of the house, the front door slamming behind him. Ruby and Vee jump up, but I wave my hand. "Leave him to me." Ruby nods and wraps her arms around Vee's shoulders.

I leave the house and walk out onto the empty street. There's a fresh earthy smell left behind from the thunderstorm. It's warm but I can't stop shivering. I head straight to the park, and it's empty except for a solitary shadow on the swings. Taking a swing next to Elliot, I stay quiet and kick the dirt with my feet till he decides to speak. It's time like this, I desperately wish I was the brother blessed with words.

"I thought it was my mum. I thought that was my mum they were lifting in the back of an ambulance zipped up in a bag. Then I see her at the door and I'm so happy she's alive. But I'm confused, who's in the bag? And she tells me it's Tom. Tom's dead. He's *dead*." He shakes his head. "I'll never see Tom again. Ever. That's it." His knuckles turn white as he grabs the metal chains harder and shakes his head violently from side to side as if to throw the reality of tonight off him. "How do you get your head around the finality of that? How do I accept that I will never, ever, see him again?"

"I don't—"

"Why bother?" He interrupts and stands, talking to the empty space in front of him. "Why bother?" He repeats, spitting the words out, spinning and looking at me for the first time. His face is pale and angry. "No matter what you do, it doesn't matter, people like me, people like *us*, will always get hurt. If we even think for one second that things might be okay, life will always put us back in our rightful place." He raises his arms in the air. "I give up!" He clenches his fists. "He's gone!" His voice is even louder. "He's gone and I can't do anything to fix that. There's absolutely nothing I can do to change that fact. He's gone. Tom is gone." He looks up at the sky and I remain quiet, annoyed that I still can't find the right words to say.

"I'm sorry," I mutter. "I don't know what to say to you."

"What do we have here? Lover's tiff?" Two figures appear out of the darkness, Lewis and Freddie standing side by side, bottles of beer in their hands. I get off the swing and place myself in front of Elliot.

Elliot pushes me out of the way and laughs out loud. "Course!" He shouts, hysteria in his voice. "Course! This is exactly what should happen tonight. This is *exactly* how my life should go! I understand this life. I *live* this life. What I don't understand are cruel moments of hope. Moments that might, for one tiny second, give me the impression that something good will happen. What do you want, Lewis? Please enlighten me. I'm dying to know. Do you want to say some cruel words? Do you want to impress Freddie there, and make yourself feel powerful and less worthless?" I clench my fist, ready to hit either of them if they make a move towards Elliot. I don't care about Freddie and his reputation; Elliot won't suffer more tonight. Lewis seems unnerved. I can tell. He's never seen Elliot like this. I keep my eye on Freddie and the bottle of beer in his hand. Elliot and Lewis stare at each other. Elliot takes a small step forward and I notice a slight hesitation in Lewis.

"You freak. Go back to your little domestic." Lewis starts to walk away.

"Did you enjoy your little dip at the reservoir? A bit too much to drink I'd say!" Freddie looks at me and laughs before they both slither off into the darkness.

Elliot's shoulders drop and he looks my way and shakes his head. "What do I do, Josh? I can't change this. I love-loved him. Oh God! He's past tense. Tom's past tense. He was there on my first day of school, he taught me how to ride a bike, and brought me to these damn swings. Josh?" he cries. "What do I do now? Tell me! I'm *actually* asking you, what do I do?"

I put my arm around him, and he rests his head on my shoulder. "I'm not very good with words but I suggest you go home, go to bed, and wake up tomorrow. For now, that's all you can do."

CHAPTER TWENTY-FOUR

ELLIOT

"Here you go." I hand Mum a cone of chips from Mr Smith's. "No salt and a waterfall of vinegar, just as you like it."

"Thank you, but I'm not very hungry, maybe I'll save them for later." She places the bag of chips by the side of her.

I sit next to her on our bench near the cenotaph in the village square. "Do you know something?"

"What?" Mum takes a drink of her Diet Coke.

"I don't have many memories of us two being outside our house when I was young, but the ones I do have are mainly sitting on this bench, playing Name the Secret." She smiles and we sit in silence. I notice she's not wearing any make-up and she's been wearing the same dungarees and grey top for three days now. "How are you feeling Mum? Honestly."

She pats my leg. "I'm okay. A little tired but I'm fine."

Mum wasn't feeling very well this morning, so I agreed to get most of the jobs done myself, collected death certificates from the offices above the library, spoke to the funeral directors, booked the church in Farnham where he married Edna and the community centre for the wake, picked hymns, ordered service sheets, and chose the readings. I pop a chip in my mouth and Mum nudges me, pointing to a man in a long, black coat across the street, talking loudly on his mobile phone.

I smile. "That man is a private investigator, hired by Ethel at the Post Office because she suspects her husband is having an affair with Edith from the Bingo Hall."

Mum smiles and nods. "Good one!"

It's been a week since Tom died, I've *got through* each day. I get out of bed, get dressed, go to school, eat lunch in the library and walk home. I've avoided as many people as possible. It's easier that way. I can look after myself and Mum. I've completed homework, cooked food, washed up, and tried to sleep. I don't sleep very well, but I'm going through the routines and feel nothing except a constant ache in my chest. I never knew grief could cause physical pain. It feels like someone's sitting on my chest, and all day I resist the urge not to double over and curl up in a ball. I haven't cried yet. Mum keeps asking if I'm okay and Josh is constantly messaging me, but I don't know why I haven't cried yet. My brain's telling me that Tom has died, and I won't see him again but that's it. It seems too big to process so my brain gives up and shuts down. I get up, create a list of jobs, and work my way through them. I know Mum's worried; she's asking me too many times if I'm okay and I'm running out of different ways I can reassure her that I am. A young couple passes, arguing loudly with each other. Mum catches my eye and I nod in their direction. She leans back on the bench, eyes narrowing, taking another sip of her drink. "Easy one. She wants fish for dinner, and he wants steak."

"That's it? That's all you're going with? All the secrets in the world and you decide they're fighting about food. You're rusty at this game, Miss Hart!" Placing the chips down on the bench, I look at the list in my jeans pocket, mentally ticking off the jobs in my head. "We need to invite people to the funeral, Mum. I know where Tom kept his address book. I could look through that?" The pain in my chest expands when I picture an empty church. "He needs people there." Mum agrees and we discuss inviting some of the neighbours and asking them to help with the food for the wake. "I've ticked off most of the jobs."

She yawns and squeezes my hand. "One more thing, and you can say no if you want." I look across to her. "The eulogy? You knew him better than anyone but, and I mean this, there's no pressure, especially with your nerves when speaking publicly." My chest hurts again thinking of the countless memories I have with Tom, playing cards, watching quiz shows, eating biscuits, learning how to play the guitar. "It's too much. I knew it. Sorry love. I shouldn't have asked."

"I'm glad you asked but give me some time to think about it. I don't want to get up there and be a nervous mess, he deserves better than that."

"He loved you, nervous mess or not, but of course you should think about it, there's no need to decide yet." Mum continues. "I'm really sorry about the talent show and the scholarship. What will happen now?"

"I doubt I'll be offered the scholarship when I sung one line and ran off the stage and unless you have six thousand pounds hiding in your bank account, plan B it is!" I smile weakly.

"What is plan B?"

"I haven't got there yet."

She squeezes my hand. "I'm so sorry."

"Not your fault. There are lots of other things I can look into, and I promise, it's fine." I lie. Her phone beeps and a smile spreads across her face, she sits up straight.

"Clint?"

She quickly puts the phone back in her pocket, but the dippy smile remains. "I'm sorry."

"Don't be sorry, Mum. I've been really selfish. You must get lonely and what with your parents leaving you when you were young and being trapped in that house. You're allowed, you deserve, a friend or even a—"

"He's not anything! Right now, he's simply a friend who makes me happy. He was asking after you and offering to help organise the funeral in any way he can. Look," she turns my chin to face her, "After what I've been through, I'm not going to rush into anything with anyone, but Clint's a kind man who makes me feel ... safe."

There's an old couple opposite us, holding hands and sharing a sandwich. It starts to feel a bit silly being jealous of Clint. Losing Tom is real hurt and worry. Why wouldn't I want Mum to be happy? Especially after all she's been through. The elderly man opposite pulls out a flask and pours them both a hot drink. "You need to invite him to the funeral."

"Are you sure?" She can't help but hide her smile.

"Yes. Invite him. It's been us two for so long and I was confused and worried you might get hurt again, but we can't let the past affect us. Invite him, but if he does anything ..." I flex my muscles and we laugh. She replies to his message, and I look at my phone.

Mum nudges me. "What about you? Have you spoken to Felicity since ... that night."

I stare at the phone screen, not sure if the pain in my chest is grief or the fact that Felicity is completely ignoring me since last week. I shrug. "She hasn't been in touch. I see her at school, and it looks like she wants to speak to me, but she turns and walks the other way. No scholarship, and now the girl I thought liked me is treating me like I'm a ghost." I rest my head on her shoulder and watch the pigeons fight for scraps of food on the floor. "Mum?"

"Yeah?"

"I do miss him."

"Me too."

We sit and watch the crowded square in silence.

CHAPTER TWENTY-FIVE
JOSH

"Can I get you anything?" Elliot's mum pops her head around his bedroom door. "Juice? Biscuits?"

"Mum!" Elliot's eyes widen. "Leave! We're fine." I arrived at Elliot's house this evening under the pretence that I want to revise for the exams together but it's really because he's avoiding everyone at school. I know he's back to hiding in the library at lunch. Elliot tests me for the thousandth time on our English texts and he can't hide his surprise when I get them all correct. We move on to ratio, Pythagoras, and trigonometry. He takes his time explaining it to me and instead of losing my head when I don't get it the first time, he gives me space to prowl his room, eat one more chocolate digestive that his mum sneaked in, sit back down on the chair by his desk and we go through it all over again.

"You're doing great," he exclaims. "What's different?"

"I have an official dyslexia diagnosis now and I've accepted the fact that I was born different."

"See! One of a kind!"

"Marshall's helping me with some revision strategies too. It's weird once I accepted that it would take me longer to complete tasks, it seemed to take some of the pressure off. For example, if I was building something in technology, I wouldn't rush it and make mistakes. If my brain works differently maybe I need to be kinder to it! Take my time. Look over stuff again. Definitely don't compare myself to others—especially you!" He throws a book at me. "Once I stopped putting so much pressure on myself to be like everyone else, it does feel a bit easier. I suppose I'm less frustrated because I know why I find things harder and it's not my fault."

"That's great." He smiles. "Should we go through it again?"

"Enough for now." I lean back in the chair. "My poor dyslexic brain can't take any more tonight." There's a painting of a windmill on his wall. "Did your mum do that one too?"

"Yeah."

"She's really good."

"I know. She's started selling some now with the help of her friend and I think it's time she had her own workshop. There's not much space in this house. There's a building in the village, near your Mum's shop actually, that's been empty for a couple of years now. That would be perfect, but she just tells me to shush when I talk about it. We don't have the money for drama courses or workshops. Who knew dreams were so expensive!" Elliot organises his revision cards, in coloured order, and lies back on his bed. "You've been a star pupil tonight, Josh McBride. I'm very impressed."

"I feel like I should attend meetings. My name is Josh McBride and I am dyslexic." I take a bow and look at the guitar. "I'm still waiting to hear you play that by the way."

His face falls. "There doesn't seem any point now, what with that night at the talent show and Tom not here anymore."

"You should keep playing. He would want that, and I need to hear this mysterious song you've written! How are you feeling about Tom and the funeral? I haven't seen you around school much lately. Are you okay?"

"I'm not sure what people want me to do. I think it would be easier for my mum if I cried and she could hug me and tell me it'll all be okay but ..." He shrugs. "I don't feel like crying. I feel a little pissed off with the world if I'm honest."

I stare out of the window. "I get that. Did you go to the meeting tonight? Was Ruby there?"

He looks over and smiles. "What's the interest in Ruby? Yep. It was a nice meeting actually. The others were supportive about Tom and the talent show, and Glenn asked us to write a letter to other young carers, saying what advice we would give them."

"And? What did you put in?"

"I said that I wish I'd told someone earlier. If I had mentioned how tough it had gotten at home earlier maybe things would have improved earlier but you don't know how things are going to turn out, do you?"

My phone vibrates in my pocket. It's Ruby.

Goodnight x

"Let me guess who that is." Elliot lies back on his bed and looks up at the space mobile on his ceiling, which seems to be the only geeky space thing to stay since I was last here a couple of Christmases ago. "I'm," he carries on with a stupid smile on his face, "seeing red hair, Doc Martens, heart of gold."

I get up off the chair and punch him on the leg. "Leave it. Nothing's happening with her anyway."

He laughs. "With who?"

I throw my Macbeth book at him. "Stop it!"

"You've kissed though?"

I blush. "Yeah, once."

He sits up. "I knew it!"

I fail to tell him it was the night Tom died. "I was thinking." I hide my face in embarrassment. "I was thinking of asking her to the prom."

Elliot stands up and claps his hands. "Yes! I love this, ask her on a date first! A picnic? Cinema? Train to Cruxby? No! There's an Italian restaurant in Farnham near her house. She mentioned it once, Bella something, said that she always wanted to go but her dad was too busy and having spaghetti with three bratty brothers didn't appeal to her. Go there! Message her now!"

"Okay, cupid. Calm down!"

I pick up my phone and type, deleting each message.

~~Are you free soon?~~

~~Do you like pizza?~~

~~Hey, fancy some spaghetti?~~

"What's up?" Elliot offers his hand out. "I can check the spelling if you're worried."

I throw my phone on his bed. "Ha! That's the least of my worries. I don't know what to say without sounding like a weirdo or a creep."

Elliot picks up my phone and hands it back to me. "Let's not overthink this, that's *my* job. Why don't we keep it simple and say ... do you want to go on a date with me?"

"Arghh! Seriously? As simple as that? What if she says no? I can't do it!"

"Josh McBride! I've never seen you like this! You've kissed, she still wants to hang out with you even though her first impression was a drunken mess diving into a reservoir! And what have we said about being scared? Send the message now before I send her one saying you love her and want to have her babies!"

I snatch the phone off him and type.

~~Would you like to go out with me?~~

~~I really like you~~

> Fancy going out on Sat?

Closing my eyes, I press send and she replies quickly.

> Yes! Elliot too?

> No. Just me and you.

We both watch the phone and wait for it to beep. It does.

> Sounds perfect x

I lean back in the chair and stare at the kiss at the end of her message before Elliot reads her response and cheers. "I feel sick to the stomach. That was awful."

"Awww. You really like her. It's cute."

I spin around on the chair. "Enough from you. Anyway, change of subject, let's talk about you and ... Felicity?" Elliot's expression suddenly changes, and he starts flicking through a book on his bedside table. "You avoiding her?"

"No! She's avoiding me."

"Come on you two! I want to bang your heads together. You're perfect together."

"Was perfect," he mumbles. "We *were* perfect together."

CHAPTER TWENTY-SIX

ELLIOT

Turning the key slowly in the lock, I step into Tom's hallway. The smell, *his* smell, hits me straight away, a mixture of furniture polish and Old Spice aftershave. Mum insisted we do this together, but I convinced her I was fine, preferring to be on my own to choose Tom's funeral outfit. It's silly picking clothes for someone who's going to be lying dead in a coffin, but he would want to look smart, even on his funeral day. The pain in my chest is still there. A crushing pain. The last few days have been busy preparing for our final exams and Tom's funeral. Tom's house provides silence, but the enormity of standing here without him weighs heavy on each breath I take. I creep through the hallway, like I'm in a museum, too scared to speak loudly or touch anything in case it breaks. I feel I could break if someone touched me. For a moment, I indulge myself and picture him, sitting in his green threadbare armchair, shouting for me to put the kettle on and asking how my day at school had been. I close my eyes and allow memory upon memory to sweep over me, each one wrapping me up in a warm hug, memories of decorating his Christmas tree, memories of him helping me with my Maths homework, memories of listening to his stories from the war or when he first started *courting* Edna. I can't believe this is all I have left.

Memories.

There'll be no new memories and memories fade. It's what they do. Time moves on. That's a guarantee. What do I have left then? Some hazy images of a man I used to know? My eyes close tight. I'll never hug him again. I'll never try to get my arms around his waist or kiss his cheek goodnight when it turns dark outside. He'll never be able to teach me a new song on the guitar or listen to my ramblings about Felicity or the drama course. Eventually, I open my eyes, the indulgent seems like punishment now, and I step into his kitchen.

Oh God!

Everything's exactly like it was when he ... collapsed. A small China plate with crumbs on it by the sink, a half-drunk mug of tea starting to curdle by the microwave. The calendar on the wall with *Elliot's Talent Show* written in black marker. He's a dentist appointment next Monday which I need to cancel. I roll up the sleeves on my jumper and begin cleaning, scrubbing the dishes, wiping the kitchen tops, and tidying the living room. I clean till my arms ache, fetching the vacuum from under the stairs and hoovering the plum-coloured carpets, polishing his shelves and each individual picture frame of Edna. The cherry blossom tree outside has started dropping its leaves, small pink snowdrops float in the evening air. There's a slim white envelope resting behind a picture frame on the fireplace with my name on it in Tom's handwriting. My finger traces the edge of the envelope before I build up the courage to open it. My heart's beating hard. There's a picture of a brown bear holding a banner saying CONGRATULATIONS! My hands shake as I open the card.

Dear Elliot,

I knew you could do it! Congratulations for being the best act at the talent show - drama college here you come! There's no stopping you now.
Your dearest friend,
Always.
Tom x

My body jolts and I fold in the middle, slide onto the carpet, and curl up in a ball, holding the card close to my chest and cry. Big, heaving sobs. I want him here. I want him back. I want him to hug me and tell me everything's going to be okay. My head pounds. "Come back, Tom." I stutter. "Please, come back." I lay curled up on the carpet until the tears stop and I'm left silent, numb, and exhausted.

I stare at the patterns on the ceiling before heaving myself upright and heading upstairs, collecting his address book on the way. In his bedroom, there's a framed wedding photo of him and Edna, and a Wilbur Smith book on his bedside table with a bookmark in. A book he will never be able to finish. I grab it, determined to find out the ending for him and open the oak wardrobe, choosing a cream-coloured shirt he wore on Sundays, a dark green jumper, and black trousers. I spend too long deciding if he needs a belt. At the bottom of the wardrobe, there's a shoebox with IMPORTANT written in black felt tip. Sitting on the floor and leaning against the bed frame, I place the box on my lap, running my fingers across his lettering before opening it up.

I handle each item with care, medals from the war, a marriage certificate, black and white photos of him as a boy and with Edna on different holidays, some at the beach and others sitting at cafes on cobbled streets. At the very bottom, is a small brown envelope which reads *To Elliot*. I open it up.

My dearest boy,

If you're reading this, I imagine I've passed on, or you're rooting through my things! If it's the former, don't cry for me. If it's the latter, get out! I had a good life—made better having you as my closest ally. I'm with Edna now, my one and only. Live your best life Elliot my boy, you've faced many challenges and always confronted them with strength and dignity. You deserve the very best but work hard to achieve all your dreams.

Talking of dreams.

I'll get to the crux of the matter.

At the bottom of this letter, I've given the contact details of Richard Brealey, a solicitor in Farnham. He's a copy of my will. Elliot, I leave my savings, house and car to you and your mother. You two showed me love and kindness, at times when you had every right to be bitter and angry with the world. Without you two, loneliness would have plagued my final years but because of the small, ginger haired boy who appeared at my front door many years ago, I got to teach someone to ride a bike, open presents with a family on Christmas day, attend school plays and even be called into school when you were in trouble! I got to teach someone how to tie shoelaces and catch a ball. I got to be a grandfather. You gave me companionship. The only thing you really need in this life. You gave me a purpose to get up each morning, especially after Edna passed on. I'll never be able to truly show my gratitude, but I hope that both of you accept my gift, and it makes the path towards your dreams that little bit easier.

As C. S Lewis would say, 'There are far, far better things ahead than any we leave behind.'

All my love dear Elliot. Always.
Tom x

My cheeks are damp, and my head hurts. I close my eyes until the grandfather clock downstairs tells me it's ten pm. Gathering all his belongings, I walk out onto the street and stare up at the night sky, finding the brightest star. "Goodnight, Tom."

CHAPTER TWENTY-SEVEN

JOSH

I stand awkwardly in the doorway of our living room whilst Mum smiles proudly. "Well, look at you." She comes over and straightens my collar, kissing me on the cheek and sniffing the air. "You look very handsome and treated yourself to some aftershave I notice."

Coral wriggles her hips in the middle of the room whilst blowing kisses into the air. "Joshy's got a girlfriend! Joshy's got a girlfriend!"

Mum gives her *the look*, and then hands me a twenty-pound note. "This one's on me. You deserve it. Back by ten, though. No later with your exams coming up."

The bus into Farnham is hot and I constantly check my armpits for sweat patches. I've arranged to collect Ruby and take her to Bella Italia, where I've booked a table for two at 7:30pm. Following Ruby's instructions, I get off at the bus stop outside the Co-op at the bottom of the hill and walk up to her house. The whole journey here I've fought my nerves, contemplated chickening out, convinced myself that no girl's worth this feeling, checked and double checked if I have sweat patches, even contorted myself into a weird position to try and smell my own neck to see if Mum is right about too much aftershave. What if I've put too much on and she collapses from the fumes before I even say hello? I arrive outside a house with three small bikes discarded on the overgrown lawn. Number 26. This is the one. The noise inside the house is familiar, shouting, running, arguing, fighting. It's oddly comforting. Knocking quietly on the door, I stand tall. The noises get louder and a young boy, with messy red hair and a big, toothless smile, opens the door.

"Err – hi, is your sister in?"

"RUBY!" He slams the door shut in my face.

It reopens and Ruby's standing there, wearing cut off denim shorts and a Pink Floyd T-shirt. Her feet bare. My heart sinks, either she's changed her mind or Bella Italia's dress code is lax. Another boy's hiding behind her leg. She's holding a tin of baked beans and rolls her eyes. "I'm so sorry. Change of plan. Can we reschedule? My dad's phoned, he has to work late, some crisis over in Cruxby." She nods to her little brothers. "There's no one to watch these three monsters."

Shouts come from inside. "Ruby! I'm hungeeee!"

She opens the door wider. "Look, come in but excuse the —" she stops and smiles. "You look very handsome." The house is manic, three small boys tear through the rooms, climbing on settees, hitting each other with cushions, all half-dressed and slightly feral. "I never usually let people past the front door, but you must understand we come as a package, me and the three terrors. There's a return policy on the package if you change your mind." She smiles. "It's organised chaos here. Mum's sleeping upstairs and these three," she scoops two up in her arms as they run past and sits them at the kitchen table, "will be in bed once they've had their supper and a bath." One brother charges in, launching himself at the chair, nearly toppling over with it.

I laugh. "If your brothers met my sisters, I reckon they could take over the world!"

She smiles whilst buttering a tower of toast and placing it on the table, a blur of grubby hands dive in. There's a moment of peace whilst their mouths are stuffed with food. Ruby grabs my shirt and places her face close to mine, I put my hands on her hips and try to slow down my breathing. "I really am sorry, but plans are not easy to keep in this house. I can't tell you the number of cancelled birthdays, holidays, Christmases, we've had because Mum's too ill, or Dad's been called into work." I kiss her lightly on the lips, she stops talking and smiles. "What was that for?"

"Because you're amazing, that's why." She blushes and turns away.

"More toast! More toast!" The boys chant, banging their forks on the table.

Her shoulders sink. "We do need to reschedule though. I can do next week? If my dad can get the—"

"How long till these three are in bed?"

She looks to her watch. "Forty minutes but I can't leave them—"

I kiss her again. "You get them to bed, and I'll be back." I steal another kiss before heading outside.

———

Lighting the strawberry Air Wick candle with a match, I stand back and admire my handiwork. One trip to the local Co-op at the bottom of the hill and I've managed to create Spaghetti Bolognese with garlic bread. It might not be as good as Bella Italia's, but it doesn't look inedible. I even managed to steal a pink rose from a bush in her neighbour's garden and put it in a pint glass. The commotion of bath time has quietened down, and I can hear Ruby reading an edited, shortened version of Jack and the Beanstalk. Their kitchen's small and easy to navigate. A long line of medicine sits next to the jars of flour and sugar.

"Oh!" Ruby is in the doorway, hand to her mouth. Her face crumples. "What the hell is this?"

I reach for her hand and lead her to the table, pulling out a chair. "I've brought the restaurant to us. Bella a la Josh! Tuck in!"

She steadies herself on the table and sits down slowly. "No-one's ever done anything like this for me before, usually the terrible three and dying mum scare anyone away before they step one foot inside this madhouse."

I take a seat opposite her and pour an orange juice from the jug. "It's a good thing I'm not easily scared then."

We eat the food and chat effortlessly about our families, school, Elliot, Tom, Steve, and my infamous trip to Cruxby. She's sitting her exams at Farnham High, going on to do A-levels in Art, English and Psychology. She wants to have a job where she can help other young carers. She also tells me she's been researching dyslexia. "I know what it is now." She looks to the ceiling. "The unique ability to see things differently in a world where most people see everything the same! And guess what?"

I smile. "What?"

"Did you know half of NASA's employees have dyslexia?"

"Hmm ... you might need to lower your expectations a little there. More chances of me working at Nandos than NASA."

I ask about her mum, but she shakes her head as if to say *not tonight* so I change the subject and tell her my worries at failing the exams, even with all the support, how I have nightmares of Mum and Marshall's disappointed faces when they realise that I was plain dumb all along and it's nothing to do with the dyslexia.

"You're worrying about stuff that hasn't even happened yet. If you go into each exam and do your best, what more can you do?"

"I know. I've started to accept that if I give my exams a hundred percent, then that's okay and even if it doesn't get me a high grade … that's okay too. It's weird … I'm more comfortable with myself than I've ever been, and I now look at things and say to myself I need to do that differently, I'm dyslexic."

"See! I'm proud of you. If anything … you're going to have more resilience than some of the others." She shrugs her shoulders and I reach out my hand and grab hers. I want to kiss her again. I stand, pull her up from the chair and cup her face in my hands, kissing her softly, exploring her lips with mine, her body relaxes, and I pull her in tighter, kiss her harder. I place soft kisses on her neck, and she slides her nails through my hair before pushing me away, cheeks flushed. "My dad's due back any minute and he's a little overprotective. I do want you to meet him but maybe another time, eh? This," she points to the table, "Was incredible. *You* are incredible."

I help her clean up and she walks me to the front door, our hands held tightly. She puts her arms around my neck and smiles. I look down at her.

"What?" she asks.

My cheeks grow hot. "Can I ask a question?"

"Yes."

"Will you go to the prom with me?"

CHAPTER TWENTY-EIGHT

ELLIOT

We both stand behind our front door. Mum in a knee length black skirt that she keeps fidgeting with and a green shirt, her hair twisted into a messy bun on top of her head. Me, in my school trousers, white shirt and black tie I stole from Tom's wardrobe. The hearse is waiting patiently outside. I saw it from the living room window, along with the wickerwork coffin I chose out of the catalogue at the funeral directors.

And Tom.

Obviously.

I grab Mum's hand. "Are you going to be okay? All the people?"

She squeezes my hand. "Today's not about me."

She opens the door and steps out first, our hands holding each other tightly. It's a beautiful spring day, a clear blue sky with a white kiss left behind by passing aeroplanes. The cherry blossom tree opposite is now bare, long thin branches reaching out like monster's arms. The driver, wearing a black suit and hat, steps out and stands respectfully by the car. Tom's letter is in my trouser pocket. I haven't told Mum about it yet. We walk slowly towards the end of the path, our hands still attached, walking sideways like a crab. I see Josh first, dressed in a black suit, and smiling. Ruby's with him. It's the first time I've ever seen her in a skirt, paired with a black shirt and a pair of Doc Martens. They're holding hands and look good together, comfortable, like they've been a couple a long time. Josh and Ruby smile at each other and look my way.

A strange man walks up the street to our left, tall, confident with a kind smile, black unruly hair with specks of grey. He doesn't take his eyes off Mum. Clint. Mum drops my hand and Clint eagerly grabs both of hers in his, they look at each other and I appear to be a shadow now. He notices me and says, "Elliot. I've heard so much about you. I'm so sorry about Tom. He sounded like a true gent."

"He was," I mutter.

He extends his hand for me to shake, which I do. Faint lines around his eyes crease when he smiles, and his nose seems too large for his face but there's something sincere about him.

"Shall we do this?" The driver interrupts and instructs that we need to follow his hearse to St. Wilfrid's Church outside of the village.

"How are we meant to do that? We can't squeeze in with Tom!"

Mum straightens up. "I've had a plan but only if it's okay with you." She nods to Tom's battered and beloved Volvo still sitting outside his house. The same car that's delivered me to school, doctor's appointments, and hospital visits. The chest pain resurfaces again. "Clint can drive it." Mum continues. "But it's *your* call." I nod, unable to speak in case an embarrassing squeak comes out. Mum kisses the top of my forehead and we head to Tom's car. Ruby and Josh are still loitering outside number 32. I call them over and soon all five of us are squished into his car. It smells of him. Mum and

Clint in the front, us three in the back, Ruby squeezed in the middle. We laugh at the absurdity of it. It feels good to laugh. Josh puts an arm around Ruby. Mum and Clint steal glances when they think I'm not looking.

I feel more alone than ever.

The car doesn't start and I show Clint what Tom used to do with the gears; he listens patiently and on the third attempt the car stutters into action. Following the hearse down Ivygreen Road, Ethel from No. 14, Mr and Mrs Thompson from No. 8 and Glenda from No. 5 are all standing outside their houses, heads bowed. Even Mr Carter, the grumpy man from No. 3 who's covered his front door with a list of people who are not welcome is standing by his gate, flat cap in hand.

Ruby squeezes my hand. "How are you feeling?"

"I'm okay." I lie. I feel like I'm going through the motions, an actor on stage, saying his lines dutifully and moving to the next scene in the script: home, car, church, wake, home. My lines are already rehearsed.

I'm doing okay.

Yes, he was a great man.

Yes, he will be sorely missed.

If I allow myself, for one tiny moment, to really digest what today's about, that I'm saying a final goodbye to Tom, the man who brought me up, who showed me the outside world when my mum couldn't, well ... it'll be too much. If I allow for one second that dreadful reality to creep in, it'll be a feeling so intense that it would crush me like a huge wave, and I'd be unable to put on this mediocre performance.

So, for now, I've a part to play.

We drive slowly through Mallowbank, memories of Tom appear at each corner, the park he took me to as a kid, the large fields near the dog's home where the fair would set up each year, where we would eat hotdogs and walk side by side, me pretending he was my grandad. Mr Smith's shop where Tom would give me twenty pence to go and buy some penny sweets. I always tried to explain to him that penny sweets didn't exist anymore, but he wouldn't have any of it. I shake my head, not wanting the memories and emotions to become too powerful, too consuming. Ruby squeezes my hand again. We remain in silence on the journey to church and I notice Mum's hand stays on Clint's leg for the whole time.

"Wow." Josh remarks as we pull up outside the church. "Look at all the people. My mum wanted to pass off her apologies, but she couldn't get the day off work." There's a mass of men and women standing on the grassy verge, many with grey hair or no hair at all, some with medals pinned to their suit jackets. I see the familiar faces of George, who's holding his cap in his hand and Frankie standing next to him. Glenn's behind them.

Mum turns around, her hand still on Clint's leg. "Who are these people?"

"Some friends from the Young Carers are here but I'm not sure about the rest. I phoned a few people from his address book, but many had moved or ... died. Maybe word's got round." I spot a few people who live on our street too.

Mum leans back and squeezes my leg. "Let's do this."

The service goes well. 'The Rose' by Bette Midler is played on the piano as Tom's carried in. I didn't tell anyone why I wanted this song, but I hope Tom would be smiling and happy now he's with his peach rose. The church's half full and the vicar delivers a speech about Tom's life, based on the information we knew, his time in the army, his job as a post clerk, and how he met Edna on a blind date at the cinema. We sing hymns, helped by the deep voices of the old men at the back, and soon the vicar calls me to the front to deliver the eulogy. I stand at the lectern and scan the church pews. Reaching for the paper in my pocket, I unfold it. My mouth's dry, and my heart's beating too fast. Memories of the audition and the talent show haunt me. I keep my eyes fixed on the wickerwork coffin, let the crowd fade away, and begin.

"Please forgive me as I indulge what Thomas Theodore Brown meant to my mum and I." My voice's wobbling but I keep my eyes fixed on the coffin. "Tom, I need to say thank you to *you*. The reasons why I'll be grateful for having you in my life are endless, but I'm going to try and share a few with your friends and family today. Firstly, you fixed the toilet when it sounded like a jet plane was landing on our roof." A few titters from the congregation and my shoulders creep down from my ears. "You taught me how to play card games and if I ever get to Vegas, I'll tell them my friend Tom can be thanked for teaching me how to hustle. Thank you for taking me to the fair every year. Thank you for helping me build a bird box for my technology project. Thank you for letting me sloth out on your settee and watch quiz shows whilst stuffing my face with custard creams. Thank you for helping me understand the Pythagoras theorem, but most of all—" The church doors open, a few heads turn, and Felicity appears like a little church mouse, scurrying to the back pew and taking a seat. I lose my place and the silence in the room weighs heavy on my shoulders as I scan the words in front of me. "But-but-but most of all ..." I ignore the sheet and look at Mum in the front row, sitting up straight, stoic, and smiling. "But most of all I want to thank you for never judging me, never trying to fix Mum or I, but remaining our rock each and every day. You were always so patient." There's a painful lump in my throat and I struggle to get the next few words out. "You-you- were always so kind, whilst other curtains twitched and closed their doors on us, you opened your front door with wide arms and a smile. When I had no one on the outside, you were there, as my dad, grandad, confidante, but most of all ..." Tears escape and I wipe them away with the back of my hand as I look back to the coffin. "But most of all you were my best friend Tom, and I'm going to miss you every single day. I hope you're up there in heaven with a cup of tea, two sugars, a custard cream and ... Edna."

Mum, Josh and Ruby clap and then stop, wide-eyed, not knowing if it is an appropriate response at a funeral. I take a seat next to Mum, who squeezes my leg and whispers. "Perfect."

Outside the church, Mum and I stand whilst a long line of Tom's friends shake our hands and offer their condolences. One man, who introduces himself as Derek Woodham, asks me about drama college and how the guitar playing is going. I wonder how a stranger knows so much about my life, but it turns out they used to play in a band together at college, Tom as lead guitarist and Derek on the drums. He informs me how most of Tom's correspondence was centred around me.

George stands in front of me, his cap still scrunched up in his hands. "I'm sorry. We wanted to be here to show that we're here for you." It's the most words I've ever heard George string together.

I wrap my arms around him. "Thank you."

Before long, Felicity's standing in front of me, her head bowed, she looks up briefly and offers me a shy smile. We look at each other and I refuse to speak first. Another old man waits patiently behind her.

"Can we talk?" she whispers.

I nod, relieved to have a moment away from the *I'm sorry for your loss* and *That was a lovely servic*e. She follows me to a wooden bench that looks out onto a small graveyard. A pot of pink carnations sits by the gravestone in front of us. Felicity takes a seat and there's a gap between us, only a couple of inches, yet it feels cavernous.

She hands me my purple cardigan. "I wanted to give you this back."

"That's why you're here?" I snap. "To give me my cardigan

back?" I'm angry and I don't know what it is. There's a rage bubbling inside of me. Am I angry at her for being absent when I needed her most? Am I angry at Tom for leaving me? Am I angry that Mum and Josh have someone to lean on? Am I angry that yet again I feel totally on my own ... again?

"I'm sorry, Elliot." Her words are soft and seem sincere.

"What are you sorry for?" My voice is strained. "Ignoring me?" My voice grows louder. "What did I do wrong?" Her head hangs and she picks at a piece of fluff on her trousers.

"You didn't do anything wrong." She shakes her head. "I tried. Honestly, I tried so many times to message you and I would pick up the phone and dial your number and then chicken out. I felt guilty, still do, for not coming after you that night, for getting a place on the course when you didn't–"

"You got on the course?" I interrupt. She continues to mess with her trousers and nods. A tear escapes. "Congratulations. You deserve that." The rage continues to bubble away inside of me.

"Thank you. I feel awful though." She reaches for my hand, but I pull it away.

"You don't need to pity me."

"You do understand I had to perform that night though? My parents. It took me months to persuade them to come to the talent show, to show them I'm serious about drama and it's not a silly hobby that *won't get me anywhere*. I wanted to show them this is what I'm good at. So ... I stayed." She puts a hand to my cheek and wipes a tear away. "You're the kindest —". I back away. "Please don't push me away."

"Maybe I've had enough of being the kind one. The good one. I don't care that you stayed at the stupid talent show, but why ignore me? You knew about Tom and how much he meant to me, yet you avoided me at every opportunity. You walked away from me in the school corridors, avoided me in class. It's easier just looking after myself. My mum has Clint now and I can go back to looking after myself." Mum's waiting at Tom's car. "I'm going to go—"

"No!" she shakes her head. "This isn't fair. I'm here now!"

"I'm sorry, Felicity." I stand up and look across the graveyard. "It's too late."

CHAPTER TWENTY-NINE

JOSH

Tutor time and Elliot's chair is empty again. Felicity's chatting to her friends in the corner, and I walk over. "Felicity?" She ignores me. "Felicity?"

She spins in her chair. "Yep? What do you want?"

I pull a chair up, sit down and lean forward. "Have you seen Elliot? I haven't seen him since the funeral last week."

"No. He's not speaking to me."

"I've never known him to have a day off in his life and he's not answering my messages and when I went round to his house there was no answer. I'm worried."

She shakes her head. "I don't think I'm the person to ask, Josh. I don't think we're ... friends anymore."

"That's not true. He really likes you. I think he's struggling—"

"He doesn't want to see me. He's made that very clear. There's nothing I can do." She turns back to her friends, and I walk away.

"Josh?" Felicity calls.

I turn around. "Yeah?"

"Thank you."

"What for?"

She smiles. "Looking out for him."

"Everyone in their seats please." Mrs Stephens stands up. "Good morning, year eleven. A lot of information to share with you today, so listen up." Elliot walks through the door and slides into the seat next to me. His head hangs low. Mrs Stephens looks across but carries on, "Firstly, your awards afternoon is in two weeks. A letter has been sent home to your parents and guardians, please make sure you bring the reply slip back in as soon as possible. It's a lovely event, a chance to celebrate all your achievements over the past five years at St. Cuthbert's."

Elliot wrings his hands together and digs his fingernail into the top of his right hand. I lean across. "Hey. You okay? I've been worried." He gives a slight nod, but his eyes remain fixed on the floor.

"Secondly," Miss continues, "Your exams are soon. We created revision timetables last week, stick to them!" Elliot pushes his fingernail down into his hand, leaving a white crescent moon shape on his skin. "Finally, before I hand out your final reports, don't forget the prom, a chance to let your hair down when all the hard work's done."

"Are you sure you're okay?" He doesn't answer me. "Elliot? What is it? Talk to me."

"Quiet please, Josh. Okay, your final reports." Mrs Stephens walks to her desk. "Usually, we send your reports home, but we decided, as it's your final one, to give you a copy too. You'll be able to see your progress in all the subjects and remember, no more second chances. Now's the time *you* take control of *your* future." She collects a batch of white envelopes from her desk and asks Anusha to hand them out before taking a seat in front of her computer. "Josh." Miss looks my way. "Can you come here for a second? I need to talk with you." I look at Lewis who's drawing on the table. What could

I be in trouble for? I can sit here silent and still find myself in somebody's bad books. I shove my chair back, edge around Elliot like he's a bomb about to explode and walk to the front of the classroom, stand at her desk, waiting for her to deliver some crap about what I'm *supposed* to have done. She studies a piece of paper in her hands. "Take a seat please." It doesn't matter how hard I try. I'll always be Josh the troublemaker, or Josh the waste of space. "I wanted to show you something—"

"I haven't done anythin' Miss." I interrupt. "Whatever anybody says, I haven't! I couldn't have worked any harder this term. I've done everythin' asked of me and more. Revised at home, used my extra time in assessments. I've—"

"Josh. Look at this." She hands me the paper. It's my latest report with my progress tracker attached. It takes me a while to work out what it all means but there seems to be more green and orange than the red car crash that was posted home last time. Actually, I check carefully but I can't see any red at all!

"There's no red, Miss!"

She laughs. "I know!"

I doubt whether I've understood it correctly and look at Miss who looks like a kid at Christmas time. "What does it mean, Miss?"

"It means, Josh McBride, you've improved in *all* your subjects. I don't know what's happened these last couple of months, but I need to tell you that I am incredibly proud of you. Whatever happens in your exams, you can hold your head up high." Her forehead creases and I wonder if she's going to give me a hug or cry but either way, I'm not sure where to look. A huge grin spreads across her face. "What did happen?"

I shrug. "Finally accepted who I was, and it seems to help! Once I accepted that I learn a different way, well it was like me, and my brain were working together instead of me getting angry with it. Nina's helped me loads and some of the teachers meet me at lunch to go through past papers - at my own speed!"

"That's great!" I keep staring at the report. "You can go now." She laughs.

I go back to my desk and Elliot's still silent and hunched over. He's opened his report and I notice two orange boxes. I don't think he's ever underachieved in anything. I desperately want to tell him that I'm doing better, the words are fizzing on my lips, about to spill over. A teacher's proud of me.

I'm proud of me!

I want to tell Mum, and Ruby. Damn it, I want to shout it to the whole class. I want to tell Marshall! I did it! All that extra work. I did it. I *can* do this.

"Elliot?" Miss has followed me to our desk. "Are you okay?" She squats down but he doesn't move and keeps looking at the floor. "Elliot?"

"I'm fine," he mutters.

"Elliot?"

"I said," his voice is louder. "I'm fine. Leave me alone, please."

She looks to me for help, but I shrug my shoulders. "Do you want to discuss—"

She reaches for his report card, but he grabs it and stuffs it clumsily into his bag before getting out of his chair and leaving the room.

I don't see him for the rest of the day.

———

That evening, I cook food for Mum and the girls. "This is nice." Mum takes a bite of her fajita. "Thanks for making it, Josh. I thought I'd be home earlier, but the shop was really busy today."

"It's fine. Coral? Want me to make you one?" She shakes

her head whilst piling a mountain of chicken onto her plate. "Mum?"

"Yes?"

"I need to show you something important."

She puts her food down and wipes her mouth with a tissue. "What is it?"

I walk over to the counter and pull my school report out of my bag. "It's from school. I'm sorry, Mum. I know I said I would try to improve, well, I need to tell you—"

She throws her tissue down and stands. "Oh, Josh. Really? This close to your exams!"

I keep a straight face. "I know."

"What in hell's name have you been up to now?" She snatches the report from my hand and reads it. Her face changes and a smile appears. "Argh! Have you seen this?" She jumps up and down, waving it in the air before showing it to me.

"Yes!" I laugh. "Mrs Stephens showed it to me in tutor time. She's really proud."

Mum wraps her arms around me and squeezes me tight. "I couldn't be prouder," she mutters.

"Mum. I can't breathe."

She releases me and skips off to show the girls. "Look, Saff. Coral! Look. Look at all this green. Your brother's smashing it." She winks at me and points a finger. "I'm so proud of you. I know it's not been easy, but I know you've been studying in your room and doing the extra revision sessions at school." She walks over to the fridge and removes a picture of a rainbow Coral drew and sticks my report up, standing back and admiring it. "It looks beautiful. I might frame it." She laughs and takes a seat back at the table.

"Mum, I made you something for always being my biggest champion even when I was a pain in the arse." I go to my bedroom and find the wooden key holder, come back to the kitchen and hand it to her. "It's to put your work keys on because well ... I'm proud of you, too."

She stands and hugs me tight again. "Thank you."

We finish eating our food, stealing smiles at each other. "Everyone must have been really proud. What did Mrs Stephens say? Does Mr Marshall know? And Elliot? Bet he sees you as competition now! What did he say?"

"Not much really. He's been missing school and walked out of tutor time today."

"That doesn't sound like him. Have you tried talking to him?"

"Yeah, but he's not answering my calls or replying to any of my messages."

"Well, keep trying." She looks at the report card on the fridge and smiles. "I'll try and call Vee too."

I pick my phone up and send another message to him.

> Talk to me.

> Please.

CHAPTER THIRTY
ELLIOT

G rabbing my old dinosaur rucksack from the bottom of the wardrobe, I sit, cross-legged, on my bedroom floor and move all my exercise books out of my briefcase and back into the bag Tom got me. The unopened letter from Cruxby Royal College of Arts falls out. It arrived a few days ago but I couldn't face seeing their rejection in print. I rip it open and read.

Dear Mister Elliot Hart,

We regret to inform you that we are unable to offer you a scholarship on the Theatre Studies course for this academic year. However, based on your references and your application, we would like to offer you an unfunded place on the course and an opportunity to come and look around the campus and meet the tutors. If you want to discuss this further, please don't hesitate to get in touch ...

I throw it on the floor. Unfunded? Which means paying for it myself. Six thousand pounds a year. Tom's letter rests by my bedside. I still haven't shown it to anyone, talking about money when he had just been buried in the ground didn't seem right, still doesn't, like I'm cashing in on his death. I hug the rucksack. "I miss you so much." My phone vibrates. Josh, again, asking me to talk to him, *again*. I pull my knees up to my chest and squeeze them tight, curl myself into the smallest ball before going downstairs to make some food. As I pass Mum's room, I can't resist a look in, hoping to see her bed made, curtains open but all I see is the same mound under the covers with some stray red curls escaping. She hasn't left the house for a week, emerging for a glass of water or a piece of toast. I can't believe we're back here again. All that hard work to be exactly where we were two years ago.

In the kitchen, I stare at the cupboard and think about what I can make with half a tin of baked beans and two Weetabix when there's a loud knock at the door. I ignore it, look at the empty fridge hoping something will magically appear. Another knock, even louder and more persistent. I close my eyes and wait for it to stop but it doesn't.

"Elliot," a deep voice comes through the letterbox, "It's Clint. Open the door please." I rest my head against the fridge door and pray for him to leave. "Elliot, please." More knocking and I hear Mum stirring upstairs. Eventually, I give in and open the door. Clint's standing there, towering over me. I wait for him to speak, too exhausted to lead this conversation. "Elliot. I don't mean to intrude but I'm worried about your mum. I've not seen her since the funeral and she's not answering her phone. Her friends at the art class are missing her too." He wrings his hands together. "Is she okay?"

"She's fine." My voice is flat, and I avoid looking at him, keeping my eyes on the streetlight as we stand in an awkward silence.

"Elliot? Can I come in? Just for a minute."

There's a moment's silence before I open the door wider. "Do whatever you want. She's upstairs, in bed. Her favourite place." He walks in, manoeuvring himself around me, and heads upstairs. "I can look after her myself you know!" I shout up behind him, sounding like a sulky child.

Clint's upstairs for a long time. There're hushed voices whilst I eat my Weetabix and stare at the same page in *Brave New World*. Mum's paintings are still leaning by the fireplace. They haven't been touched since Tom died. It's past nine o'clock when Clint finally comes downstairs and takes a seat on the settee opposite me. I stare at my book and refuse to speak, aware I'm immature but slightly enjoying it too. "Elliot, can we chat?" He comes and sits next to me. His eyes look sore. "I've had a good chat with your mum, and we're going to book a doctor's appointment for her tomorrow."

"We?"

"She admits that she's struggled this past week or two." He ignores my question. "But the thing is with depression—"

"Don't!" I jump up and he sits back. "Do not tell me what *the thing is with depression*. Don't dare sit there and tell me what *the thing is with depression*. At the tender age of sixteen, I'm an expert on it. I could write books on it. I've lived with her depression day after day. I know it all, Clint. Every sad, little detail. I know the days she hides in her bed, the days she doesn't eat, the days I spend at school feeling sick to my stomach waiting for a call to say ..." I sit back down. "Please don't come into *our* house and tell me what *the thing is with depression*."

He looks to the floor. "I'm sorry. I shouldn't have said that."

I look at him for the first time since he's entered the room and he's a blank expression I find hard to read. Mum's standing in the doorway wearing her white nightie and claret red dressing gown, she ties the cord around her waist, wraps her hair up in a bun on top of her head and takes a seat next to Clint, who reaches for her hand and squeezes it tight.

There would be a time she would sit next to me.

I'm losing her.

I've lost Tom, Felicity and now her. It doesn't matter whether it's depression or Clint. I'm losing her ... again. She looks in my direction, her face pale, and dark shadows under her eyes.

"Did you hear all that?" I mutter.

She nods. "I'm so sorry." She shakes her head and tears fall down her cheeks. Clint leans in and gently wipes them away. "I'm sorry about all those days. I'm sorry for the days that will come in the future because they will Elliot. Those days will come again." A tear falls down my cheek which I wipe away quickly. "But there will be fewer of them. Please don't worry about me. It's not like last time. Clint's made me realise—" I can't help but roll my eyes, but she continues, her voice sterner. "Clint's made me realise that I need extra appointments with Dr Jonas when I'm finding things more difficult and with Tom—"

My eyes meet hers. "You're not the only one hurting, Mum. You're not the only one missing him. I needed you and you were gone. Again. I've exams and life after exams to think about but no one to talk to. You're not the only one with things going on." Clint remains silent, his eyes fixed on the floor, both hands clasped around Mum's, part of me hates the fact he's here for this conversation, invading our privacy. I hate the fact that he made Mum realise she needed help, and it was *him*, not me, that got her out of bed. Mum, reading my mind, moves to sit next to me but I get up and stand by the fireplace. "I get you're sad. I am too. I even get this," I shake my hand between her and Clint, "but I feel—" My voice breaks and I look out of the window, stare at the illuminated fish tank in the house opposite.

"What?" Mum edges closer. More tears fall down my face. "What do you feel? Tell me how you're feeling."

"I feel alone." She goes to grab me, but I push her off and run out of the house.

CHAPTER THIRTY-ONE

JOSH

My phone vibrates. Ruby.

Any luck?

No hes not home mum said he ran off. I'm worried.

Me too. I would come over but Dad's at work.

I'll let you know when I find him.

I put my phone back in my jeans pocket and head to the park. Where the hell is he? Lewis, Freddie, and a taller, unfamiliar boy are sitting on the skate ramp. Lewis is smoking and they all have a bottle of beer in their hands.

"Oi!" I shout at them. "Have you seen Elliot?" They stop talking and stare, Freddie looks me up and down in one brief glance.

I stand up straight, push my shoulders back, maintain eye

contact, and refuse to look away. All the tricks I perfected growing up with Steve.

"Josh, hi! We meet again. How are you?" Lewis jumps off the ramp and approaches me, Freddie and the taller boy follow closely behind. They come close, enough for me to smell their beer and cigs. I keep my eyes on them, refusing to show any sign of weakness. "You're looking for Elliot?"

"Yes, I need to find him. Have you seen him?" My voice is strained.

"Oh!" Lewis laughs, looking to the others for a reaction. "You mean Matchstick! Ginger hair? Freak? What is it with you two? I see you cosying up with each other at school. Turned soft on us, Josh McBride?" He inches closer and I clench my right fist.

"Last time I saw you," Freddie interjects. "You were taking a dip in the water. It's a shame." I look at him whilst still trying to keep an eye on Lewis. I'm out numbered. "I had big plans for you." He pushes his black hair away from his eyes and flicks his cigarette into a nearby bush.

"Have you seen him?" I press on.

Lewis shrugs. "Maybe. Maybe not. What's it to you?"

"Lewis. You're pathetic. Do you know what? Leave it." I spin around and walk away, tense up, knowing what they could do to me with my back turned.

"You're an embarrassment, Josh. Waste of space. They should've left you in the water." Lewis calls. I turn around and march straight back to him. He wouldn't be saying any of this without the others to impress. Freddie and the other boy move straight to his side and I see something glint briefly in Freddie's hand.

A knife.

Memories of Cruxby flash in my mind. The park. The tree. The mugging. It feels like all four of us are holding our breath waiting for someone to make the next move, until a loud wail makes us all jump. Elliot appears. He's running across the park like a lunatic, arms windmilling, shouting at the top of his voice, "Wahhh!" Lewis and his friends are caught off guard and, in an instant, Elliot collides with them. They tumble in a heap, rolling around on the grass and I'm not sure which limb belongs to whom until Elliot jumps up, eyes wide and manic. "Run!" he shouts, and we turn and flee. I run fast, not knowing if Elliot's close behind or whether they are following us until I hear their voices.

"Get here!"

"Oi!"

"I swear to God—"

"Elliot! Run!" I race down the path. The footsteps and shouts grow louder. Elliot appears by my side, inching in front of me and we run out of the park. Their voices are even closer. I jump over a small wall but catch my foot and tumble onto the gravel path, scraping the palm of my hand across the tarmac. Elliot stops and looks behind me, his eyes wide. They're close. He runs over and grabs my hand, dragging me up. "Come on!"

I stumble to my feet, and we run, turning right onto the terraced street. There are shouts right behind me, suddenly Elliot's in front, his long legs covering more distance, looking like a gazelle you see on the animal shows.

"Freaks! Just you—" Lewis's voice is louder. I run faster, catch up with Elliot. My heart's pounding. The image of the knife stuck in my head. If they reach us, we won't escape again.

They'll hurt us.

They'll kill us.

"In here!" Elliot grabs my sleeve and pulls me into a small alleyway at the end of his avenue. We crouch down behind a green wheelie bin, our breaths rattling. Elliot starts sniggering and I put my hand over his mouth.

"Shush!" I think back to Freddie's knife. "Quiet. This is not a game. This is serious. Does Lewis know where you live?"

Elliot removes my hand and smiles. "Course, he came round for tea last night. We snuggled up and had margherita pizza together."

I smile and hit him on the arm. "You've lost your mind!" We wait in silence before it feels safe enough to creep out. "They might still be looking for us. I don't think Freddie's one to give up on a fight."

"I know a place to go," Elliot replies. "Come with me."

Elliot turns the key in Tom's front door, whilst I keep my eyes on the empty street. A black cat jumps onto his garden wall and makes me jump. Once inside, he gets us both a glass of water and we go to the living room. I close the curtains and sit down. Then we laugh and laugh, so much my stomach starts to ache. "What was that?" I wave my arms around trying to copy Elliot's banshee wailing in the park. I laugh again, holding a hand on my stomach and struggling to catch my breath.

Elliot laughs. "Might not have had style but the end result was the same! Their faces as a gangly, ginger haired kid comes railroading through the park. It was crazy. I saw them up in your face and flipped! Had enough! How dare they?" He puts his head in his hands. "Maybe I'm losing my mind."

I lean back in the chair. "Don't be silly. I think that was your finest moment, Elliot Hart. Never mind the talent show, that was an Oscar worthy performance."

His face changes and the smile vanishes as he looks at a picture of Tom and Edna on the fireplace. "What's going on with you? Tell me. Ruby says you missed the last Young Carers meeting. You've missed days of school. What's going on in that head of yours? Please tell me. I want to help." I see him fighting with himself. The words perched on the edge of his lips and then pushed back. I wait patiently. The clock ticks from the hallway until he looks at me and starts talking.

"There was a moment before the talent show where I thought everything might be okay. I allowed myself to believe in a life that was hopeful and ... maybe even a little bit carefree. Me and Felicity were getting on well. I was going to perform for a chance to get a place on my dream course. My mum and Tom were going to watch me. My mum! Who couldn't leave the house for most of my childhood was going to sit in the front row and watch me sing! I allowed myself to believe it was all going to be okay, and then ... it wasn't. The life I know so well came flooding back. I didn't perform and I let everyone down. I lost Tom. Felicity ignored me. And Mum ... she's been spending days in bed again. It's so familiar to what it was like before Cruxby. She hides and I do my best, but I'm *so* tired of doing my best and getting nowhere."

"Is your mum okay?" I remember the night she was having a seizure at Elliot's house.

"I think she will be. Clint's around there now looking after her."

"Your Mum is stronger than you give her credit for." My phone beeps. It's my mum asking where I am. I quickly reply that I'm with Elliot and will be back soon. I message Ruby too. Elliot's shoulders slouch and he rubs his forehead. "I imagine every day's a battle for your mum," I tell him. "And she wins that fight most of the time. Let her have a few days off, to regroup, recharge, reset."

He looks at the picture of Tom again. "I know."

"And you're grieving your closest friend. Give it time, stop putting so much pressure on yourself. Honestly? Once I stopped putting pressure on myself at school, it's easier. All those things that have happened to you in the past, well they've kind of equipped you with the qualities you need for the future. You're one of the strongest people I know. You'll find another course and—"

"I got in the course."

"What?"

"I got in. I didn't get the scholarship which was to be expected as I didn't actually perform!" He laughs. "But they've offered me a place except I'd have to pay for it myself."

"I'm so sorry mate. That seems extra cruel. To show you the prize you could've had."

He rubs his head. "But there's another thing that's bothering me ... I *can* afford the course now."

"Yeah? How?" His eyes keep on the picture of Tom until he eventually pulls out a letter from his jeans pockets and hands it to me, waiting patiently as I read it.

There's a lump in my throat once I finish. "Bloody hell. I wish I had a friend like him."

"I don't want to cash in on his death, Josh. I don't want to be happy because he died. It feels really wrong."

"For a clever person you're being really dumb right now. Your life's been so plagued by crap that you can't see a good thing when it's staring you right in the face." I wave the letter. "Tom wants to help you achieve your dreams. Let him! Does your mum know about any of this?" He shakes his head. "You need to chat with her. She's waiting at home worried sick about you."

"For someone who isn't so good with words ... you're doing a decent job!" I laugh. "Thanks Josh, for everything. I think I've been a bit of an arse with my mum to be honest."

I lean forward. "And ..."

"And Clint."

"And ..."

He looks at me, defeated. "And Felicity."

CHAPTER THIRTY-TWO

ELLIOT

Josh and I lock up Tom's house and I creep through my front door, the kitchen light's still on. Mum and Clint are sitting at the table, cradling mugs of coffee in their hands. I lean in the doorway, hands in my pocket. "Sorry," I mutter.

Mum rushes over and places her arms around me. "You idiot. I love you."

I look at Clint. "I'm sorry."

He smiles, his eyes creasing. "I'll put the kettle on, eh?"

"I was ... I *am* struggling. With school, Tom ... you." I look at her, my eyes filling up. I take a seat and hand Mum Tom's letter. "I need to show you this. I'm sorry I didn't show it to you sooner, but you were in bed, and I was confused and angry, but you should read it." It's quiet in our kitchen whilst Clint makes the brews and Mum reads the letter. Once finished, she folds it up neatly and continues to stare at it, tears in her eyes. "I need to tell you something else too. I didn't get the scholarship."

She grabs my hand. "I'm sorry. That's not fair. You're incredibly talented and if they could only see—"

"They've offered me a place though, based on the references from Mr Kay and Mr Owen but I would have to pay."

Mum looks at the letter and smiles. "You would have the money now. Why didn't you show me this before?"

I shrug. "I was being dumb. It felt weird talking about money so soon after his death, when all I could think about was not seeing him again."

"I understand but you know what this means?" She takes the mug from Clint. "You can get on that course; we can pay for travel or the accommodation and any equipment you might need." She reaches for my hand. "I'm heartbroken Tom isn't here now but I know he would want you to live your fullest life. That's all he ever wanted ... for us both." Mum hands Clint the letter to read.

I think back to the last couple of weeks. Mum hiding in her bedroom. "But you. What about you? I won't be around as much, especially if I stay there during the week."

"Elliot Hart. I was sad. I *am* sad. I miss Tom. He was a dad to me when my own parents disowned me. His death brought back a lot of memories and we both know they're not all good, but that does not mean I'm locking myself in a house for another ten years. I'll see Dr. Jonas this week, but you must understand I'll still have bad days but that doesn't mean it will be as bad as before and it is not your job to look after me anymore. It should have *never* been your job. I can't believe you got in! My son! The next superstar! What happens next?"

"I need to reply and accept my place on the course, but they've invited me to meet the tutor and look around the campus, and as long as I get decent grades, I'm in!"

Mum clenches her fists like an excitable child. "This is so exciting. When do you need to visit?"

"Ermm, tomorrow."

"What? But I was going to see the doctor and it's in

Cruxby—" There's fear in Mum's eyes, she still has a daily battle with the outside world. Taking the empty mugs to the sink, I look at them both. "It's fine. I can get a train in; I think I might even have a map of Cruxby somewhere."

"I'll come with you." Clint's voice is calm and comforting. "I'd be happy to help if you'd let me. We could have lunch at a café I know near the campus and make a day of it." Mum fails to hide her eagerness at this plan.

"That would be great," I reply. "Thank you. Now, it's been an eventful night and I need my bed but one last thing from me." I look at Mum. "If I allow Tom to help me achieve my dreams, you need to allow him to help you achieve yours. That art studio you've always wanted?" I raise my eyebrows.

She comes over and hugs me tight. "One step at a time, my love."

I go upstairs and collapse into bed, exhausted, and stare at the space mobile, allowing myself to imagine a future where dreams *are* possible. I look at my phone and notice a ton of missed calls from Mum, Josh, and Ruby. I find Felicity's number and contemplate phoning her but chicken out and type a message.

~~I'm sorry~~
~~I've been stupid~~
~~Forgive me?~~

> Goodnight x

I stare at the screen but there's no reply, so I stuff it under my sheets and curl up. Suddenly, the phone beeps and I frantically search for it. It's Josh.

> Always in your corner.

CHAPTER THIRTY-THREE

JOSH

I place the girls' cereal bowls down on the kitchen table and Mum comes skipping in, still wearing her tartan pyjamas. She kisses me on the cheek and roots in the fridge.

"Why are you so smiley, Mummy?" Coral asks, stuffing a top-heavy spoon of Coco-Pops into her mouth.

Mum tilts her head around the fridge door. "Because, my sweetheart, it's your brother's last day at school. Study leave starts today!" I sit next to Saff who's holding the whole bowl up to her mouth and drinking the remains of the chocolatey milk, leaving a brown moustache behind, before smiling proudly. Mum grabs a fork and tucks into last night's cold lasagne. "Let me tell you both. There were many times I didn't think your brother would make it to this day, so yes, I'm happy and yes, I'm going to celebrate!" She puts the radio on and starts dancing.

"How else would someone celebrate, but with some cold lasagne?" I ask.

She stops dancing, shrugs, takes another bite and winks. "Right, tell me the plans for today again."

"I've told you! There's an award ceremony this afternoon, where families have been invited to celebrate our achievements, but I very much doubt I'll be getting anything, so you really don't have to come—"

"I wouldn't miss it for the world. Now, you have an important decision to make. Do you want me to bring my big *I heart Josh* banner or my megaphone to cheer you on? I've already ordered the brass band and the red carpet." She laughs and finishes off the lasagne.

"Fine!" I laugh. "I give in. I'll see you there." I collect my latest piece of woodwork from the shed and say goodbye to them all.

"Bye Joshy smelly pants!" The girls sing in unison as I leave the house.

At tutor time, I take a seat next to Elliot. He's been in school every day since that night at the park last week. He smiles at me. There's excitement rippling through the room, some students have already started signing each other's shirts and drawing inappropriate images in brightly coloured felt tips. Miss has brought out two tins of Quality Street and there's music playing from the computer. I smile back at Elliot, and we join in, signing shirts and hugging fellow classmates like we'll never see them again when we're fully aware we will see them during the exams and around the village. Miss comes over to mine and writes 'so proud' in red felt tip before bouncing off to the front of the room.

"Okay, okay!" She flaps her hands. "Take a seat. I need to say a few words." We all find an empty space to sit on chairs and on tables. We look at Miss who's sticking her bottom lip out. "Now, I know we still have exams but today is a time to celebrate and say goodbyes. It's been a privilege being your form tutor for the past five years, seeing you grow into the delightful young adults sitting in front of me today." I look around for Lewis but he's not there. "I've made a little something to show how far you've all come." She goes over to her desk and clicks the computer, a video starts to play on the whiteboard, images of the tutor group appear with the lyrics of Queen's 'Don't Stop Me Now' blasting out from the speaker. The class gasp and laugh at their younger selves and questionable haircuts and fashion choices. Images of school trips, drama shows, residentials. My shoulders drop when I realise there are little photos of me and the two where I do appear, I look angry and solemn.

It's hard to see old Josh.

The class cheers as a picture of the whole tutor group winning the rounders tournament in year nine appears on the screen, a mass of smiling faces, people on each other's shoulders, arms wrapped around each other.

I'm not there.

I was in Mr Owen's office that afternoon because I threw a football at Edward Burns's head. Elliot's in the background of the picture, the only student not looking at the camera, his eyes looking at the ground, wearing a different coloured T-shirt to everyone else.

I lean into Elliot. "I'm not in any pictures."

He looks back and shrugs. "I didn't want to be in any pictures."

"Does it not get to you?"

He looks down at his shirt filled with scribbles. "Two years ago, there might have been a couple of signatures on this, Mrs Stephens included! And I would've been sitting at the back, trying to make myself invisible and you—"

"Would have been tormenting you or at the oak tree smoking with Lewis."

"I'm not invisible anymore, Josh." He doesn't look at me. "Let's not look back, eh? Let's look forward."

I put my arm around his shoulder. "Very deep and profound Mister Hart. I like it." I write *look forward* on his shirt. I know he's right and it's not healthy to have regrets, but I do. If I could do these school years again, I would do it differently, tell people about Steve, accept the help, not hurt others simply because I was hurting. The video comes to an end, and everyone claps.

"Okay, one last picture, everyone in." Miss gets her camera from the drawer and we all bunch in. I push Elliot in front of me.

"What are you doing?" He laughs.

"It's my job to make sure you are never invisible again."

"After three," Miss calls, "Shout, anything is possible! 1 ... 2 ... 3."

"Anything is possible!"

No work is completed in the morning's lessons. It's a hive of shirt signing, chocolates, music and goodbyes. I find myself hugging people I've never spoken to, a group of girls are crying and wailing about how much they will miss each other when most are attending the same college in September.

After lunch, we are ushered into the gymnasium for the awards event, chairs have been lined up in long rows and there's a large banner above the projector saying GOOD LUCK! Students are directed to sit at the front and our family and friends will sit at the back. I'm grateful that the girls will be at school and nursery, not running down the middle aisle like drugged up monkeys. There's music blaring through a large speaker in the corner, some woman asking what we have done today to make us feel proud. Marshall walks up to me. "Josh."

I stop and give a slight nod, stuffing my hands in my pockets. "Sir."

"I wanted to come over and say well done, Josh. You've made quite an impression on me. It takes real guts to change your attitude when everyone has come to expect one version of you. If you ever need anything, come and find me." He goes to walk off.

"Sir?"

He turns. "Yes?"

I drop my bag on the floor and open it up whilst he walks back. I find the piece of woodwork and hand it to him. "It's nothin' special, but I wanted to give you something to say thank you. Y'know? I didn't make it easy, but you never gave up on me." I hand him a small wooden sign with Mr Marshall engraved in it. "It's for your door."

His forehead creases. "Thank you, Josh. I'll treasure it."

"Can I ask you something, Sir?" He nods. "How's your dad?"

He keeps his eyes on the wooden sign. "He passed away."

"I'm sorry, Sir,"

"He passed away that day you told me to go and see him—"

"And, did you? Did you see him? I noticed you were missing from class."

He smiles. "I left straight for the hospital after our conversation. I was there to say goodbye. So, thank *you*."

We smile, shake hands and I scuttle off to my chair. It seems apt that I'm sitting next to Highlighter Girl after spending most of my English lessons watching her colour coordinate the inside of her pencil case. The music stops and heads turn as our family and friends are let in through the doors at the back. I see Mum with Vee and smile, roll my eyes when she gives an embarrassing wave, she might as well be shouting "Coooeee" across the crowd. Elliot's sitting in the row in front of me and we smile at each other.

Mr Owen steps up to the microphone and delivers a heartfelt speech about our next adventure and then moves onto the awards. Name after name is announced and clapped for their excellence in Science, PE, Art. "The next award goes for perseverance. A quality we admire at St. Cuthbert's High School. This award is given to an individual who puts in the effort when it feels like the hurdle might be too high. I've had a sneaky look at his latest grades, and it proves perseverance does pay off! The award for most improved is ... Josh McBride!"

CHAPTER THIRTY-FOUR

ELLIOT

Josh's mum is whooping from the back of the hall, half out of her chair. Pools of laughter and clapping spread out across the students, all eyes are on Josh, who's still sitting motionless in his chair. Harmony, from my English class, is nudging him to get up. Eventually, he stands up and edges through the tight gap between the chairs, apologising profusely for squishing on people's toes. He steps up onto stage and towers over Mr Owen, shakes his hand and takes the certificate, as he turns to leave the stage he suddenly stops and heads back to the microphone, where Sir's already started to present a trophy for our successful football team. Sir stops and they have a private conversation before Josh leans into the microphone. A piercing sound shoots around the room, and Josh steps back a few steps.

"Won't keep you long." His voice is deep and booms to every corner of the gymnasium. "But I do need to say somethin'." He pauses, and it feels like the audience has taken a breath in with him. An impromptu speech by the boy who has caused havoc for most of his time at St. Cuthbert's is captivating. I'm leaning forward, biting my thumb nail. "I haven't really been nice to some of you over the past five years, and I highly doubt I deserve any award, but that's for me to deal with, but I do need to say ... I do need to say to the teachers and you lot, Damn it. I need to say it to my mum! I'm sorry." He coughs. "I'm truly sorry. I got lost in my own troubles and I wasn't dealing with them very well. This award is for," he looks at the certificate. "Perseverance, but you can only persevere if you have people who stay by your side, especially through the tough times. There are three people in this room who stood by my side when I made wrong choice after wrong choice. My mum." A loud shout comes from the back of the room again, "Mr Marshall." I look at Sir who smiles and nods at Josh, "and to Elliot Hart." Everyone looks my way. "Thank you." There's lots of clapping as Josh walks off the stage, Mr Owen raises his eyebrows before carrying on with the accolades for the football team.

After the final award is given, a sense of restlessness comes from the students caused by numb bottoms and dead legs, and I yearn to get out into the sunshine. "If I can keep you for five more minutes," Mr Owen proceeds apologetically. Groans ripple across the audience. "There's one special award we want to give out this afternoon. One we've never given before. Earlier this year, one of our pupils found himself in difficulty at Clowbridge reservoir and hopefully, after some important lessons in tutor time, we're now fully aware of the dangers of being by open water. However, another St. Cuthbert pupil showed great courage and bravery and it is without a shadow of a doubt, his actions on that night, saved another person's life. This year we would like to give an award for outstanding bravery to ... Elliot Hart."

My legs are jelly as I make my way to the stage. I take the certificate off him, and he asks if I want to say a few words. I look out to the mass of expectant faces and my heart starts to race. I lean into the microphone. "I don't want to say much.

I'm not very comfortable up here. Never have been." My eyes stay fixed on a piece of pink chewing gum stuck to the gymnasium floor. "But I'll say this. I spent many years hiding at this school, hiding at the back of classrooms, hiding in the library, hiding in the toilets. I now know that no one should ever make you feel that you have to hide. We are all different and we all deserve to be seen." I scuttle off the stage and notice Felicity's sitting in the front row, looking up at me and smiling.

CHAPTER THIRTY-FIVE

JOSH

"Stop fussin'." I try to get out my front door whilst Mum gives me the tenth pep talk of the morning, *keep calm, read the question carefully, do your best.* It's our first exam this morning, English Language.

"Joshy!" The girls tumble down the stairs. "We've made you something." They stand together, arms outstretched, a piece of paper in each hand. Coral's drawn a picture of herself in felt tip with GUD LUK written in big, purple letters. Saff is a little more nervous and at the last second, hides her picture behind her back and shakes her head. Coral tries to encourage her, wide eyed. "Go on Saffie!" But she shakes her head again.

I crouch down to her level, and she smiles. "I'll make you a deal. I don't need to see it right now, but can you tell me what it says, it might help me today." She nods. "Go on then."

"It says I love you."

I kiss her cheek. "Thank you. I love you too, shrimpy."

Eventually, I escape the house trying to convince them that there won't be an exam to sit if I'm late. It's only half eight but you can tell it's going to be a hot day; the sky's cloudless, and the air's still. The street's quiet until I spot Ruby running in my direction. "I'm so glad I caught you." She pants, her hands on my shoulders.

I take her hands. "Good morning to you too! Why does no one seem to understand the importance of time this morning?" I look at my watch. "You've an exam to get to, too!"

She takes a deep breath and smiles, a devilish grin. "I wanted to see you and do this." She kisses me on the lips, and I fold my arms around her, bringing her in close.

"Sod it. What's a few minutes?"

She pulls away and laughs. "And I wanted to tell you good luck ... good luck!"

"Same to you." I lean in and kiss her again.

"Oh!" She waves her arms in the air. "I wanted to give you this too!" She hands me a shiny red pen from her pocket. "It's my mum's, before she got ill, she used to write. Half-finished novels everywhere in our house. She loved it. I know you use a laptop now, but I thought it might bring you luck!"

It takes me a while to speak. "You should have this, not me."

"With all the respect in the world Josh my dear, you need luck more than me!" She taps me on the head with the pen.

I kiss her again and whisper in her ear, "I think I'm falling for you, Ruby Flanagan."

Her hands grab my face. "You big softie. Now go! Show them what you've got and phone me after." And with that, she's gone, running back up the street.

On the way to school, I check my exam details again which Mrs Stephens kindly printed off on green paper for me. I need to be at the Learning Support Department at 9 am. English Language GCSE, a story to read and answer questions and then a story to write. Out of all my exams, this will be the hardest one and I have to pass it to get on my joinery course. That pressure sits heavily on my shoulders till I find myself outside the doors to the Learning Support Department. I spot Lewis walking into the main building with his mum. There's around nine of us waiting outside the small room, all restless and not looking at each other. Marshall comes striding over, mug in hand. "Good morning, everyone." He pats me on the back. "Let's get in and settled."

One of the rooms has been set up already, our papers are on the desk, there's a clock above the whiteboard and it says START and FINISH in big, black capital letters on the small board in the corner. I find my exam number on the desk and there's a laptop already there. Taking a seat, I feel quite lucky to be doing the exam in this room and not the huge, echoey gymnasium. I'm by the window and it looks out onto the hills and conifer trees. Marshall wishes us good luck at the door and then a small, elderly woman scuttles in and reads some instructions from a sheet of paper in her hand. I try not to think about the countless times I've tried to take a test and failed, all the times I've walked out or tried my best and still failed. I try not to think of the disappointed faces of Mum and Marshall if I fail this exam, but every time I try *not* to think of it, that's the only outcome I can picture. I can only picture a blank screen and me having to go home and tell Mum I didn't know what to write. The old lady informs us we can start and puts the time, 9:02, on the board. I see her brain hurting as she tries to account for the different extra times each one of us is allowed. A voice inside my head shouts. *You can't do this. You'll fail.* I roll Ruby's mum's pen in my hands and decide to do the story first, get it out of the way. Four possible titles, pick one.

The Journey
The Choice
The Wedding

The Letter

I think back to Cruxby and smile, circle The Journey and begin typing. "I sat on the train, leaving my quiet village behind me."

CHAPTER THIRTY-SIX
ELLIOT

"Time's up. Pens down please." The man at the front of the gymnasium announces. I lean back in my chair and look up for the first time since the English exam started. I think it went okay. I answered every question and wrote a short story about a boy who received a letter from his dead Grandad. We're dismissed row by row. I collect my dinosaur rucksack from the side of the room and walk out into the sunshine, searching the crowd of pupils for Felicity but can't see her. I wish we were still friends. I desperately want to know how she got on and discuss what stories we wrote. I decide to sit on the wall and wait for Josh.

"Elliot!" Josh runs over. "How did it go? I think mine went well!" He smiles. I take my tie off and roll up my sleeves, start to reply but Josh barely lets me finish my sentence before telling me about his exam, in detail, how he wrote about two boys going on a trip to the city and discovering a secret about their lives, how he finished most of the questions in section A and still had time to check his work. He's bubbling with adrenaline and relief, practically dancing around me as we walk up the road away from school. "That might be the first exam I've finished and with time to spare! I might have the looks *and* the brains now. Watch our Mallowbank!" Once he takes a breath, we decide to pop into Mr Peter's shop for an ice-cream. Josh buys a strawberry Cornetto for the homeless man sitting outside the shop and hands it to him on the way out. Leaving the coolness of the shop and walking back out into the sunshine, I spot Felicity across the street talking with two of her friends. There's a heavy feeling in my stomach, wondering how we ... how *I* got this so wrong.

"Talk to her." Josh takes a bite of his vanilla ice-cream, still grinning and on a high from his exam. "Talk to her right now. You two are good together. It's the prom soon, invite her." I stare at Felicity, wishing she would notice me and come running over, wishing we could discuss the exam and revise together, wishing we could discuss the end of *Brave New World* together. But she doesn't. "Remind me again, Elliot. What did you win an award for?" He smirks.

"Bravery."

"Do it now before it's too late."

Felicity doesn't see me and starts to walk off. "Felicity!" My voice is high-pitched. "I hate you," I mutter to Josh, who waves and walks off in the direction of his house.

She stops, turns around and sees me, her face expressionless as I jog across the street and stand awkwardly in front of her. My chocolate ice-cream melts around my hand. There's so much I want to tell her. That I miss chatting to her. That I think of her every day. That I look for her all the time, knowing my day will be that much brighter simply by seeing her. I want to tell her that we will be attending the same college. I want to tell her that I'm so incredibly proud of her for getting on the course and I'm sorry it's taken me so long to say that, but I was angry and hurt. I want to tell her that I think it takes real guts to stand up against your parents. I want to tell her that if it wasn't for her, I might not have gotten through the tough days with Mum. I want to tell her that I'm sorry for getting this so wrong. That I'm scared people I care about will eventually let me down or hurt me or ... leave me. My hand's now covered in melted ice-cream, and I've still not spoken a single word.

"Did you finish Brave New World?" I squeak.

She sighs. "Is that what you want to talk about, Elliot? The ending of Brave New World?" No, I want to grab your hand. I want to chat with you about exams. I want to kiss you. I want to ask you to prom. I want to ask you to be my girlfriend. My stomach hurts. I want to leave. I want to run away. I want to hide under my covers. She shakes her head. "I can't do this. I won't do this for you. I'm not holding your hand, Elliot. If you want to say something to me ... say it." My mouth opens but no words come out, they're all in my head spinning but I don't know what to say or how to say it. She shakes her head again. "I thought not. I made a mistake not being there when Tom died, and I have apologised for it, but I refuse to be punished anymore." She turns and leaves, as a puddle of chocolate ice-cream collects at my feet.

CHAPTER THIRTY-SEVEN

JOSH

I check my armpits one last time before taking a slow, deep breath and knocking on Ruby's front door. I'm holding some sad looking red tulips I bought from the Co-op and wearing a black suit I hired from a shop in Farnham, which now feels too tight on the waist. Familiar chaotic sounds come from inside her house until a tall man opens the door, Ruby's father. It's the first time I've met him, and I feel very small in comparison. I suddenly realise how much I want him to approve of me. "Hi. Mr Flanagan, Sir." I wipe my hand on my trousers and extend it, nervously, for him to shake, he takes it and crushes my fingers in his grip.

"Ruby!" Three cheeky faces appear from behind his leg. "There's a nervous looking boy at the door. Is he yours?" My cheeks flush and he laughs. "Come on in, son." He opens the door wider before scooping up two of the boys and leaving me alone at the bottom of the stairs. Ruby appears at the top, wearing a long black dress with a slit up the side. It hugs her figure and I suddenly feel hotter. She looks gorgeous and I can't help but feel inadequate with my droopy tulips and sweaty pits. Our eyes stay fixed on each other as she slowly takes each step in her high heels. As she approaches, I wonder how I've been so lucky to call her my girlfriend. I also wonder how long it will take before I mess this all up.

"You look beautiful," I utter. She smiles, sheepishly. A smile that makes me fall for her even more.

"Are these for me?"

I hand her the flowers awkwardly and kiss her on the cheek. "Yes."

"Thank you. Can I ask a favour?" I squeeze her hand and nod. "Will you come and meet my mum?"

I squeeze her hand tighter and answer without hesitation. "Course."

She takes off her *stupid heels* and leads me back up the stairs to a room at the front of the house. A frail looking woman lies in a grey metal bed you usually see in hospitals. The evening sun shines through the window and she appears to be sleeping. There are framed photos of Ruby with her parents and brothers on the windowsill and cabinet, along with lots of flowers that look much prettier and brighter than my pathetic tulips. Ruby walks over and grabs her Mum's hand, stroking the top of it delicately. "Mum," she whispers. "Josh is here. You know, the boy I've been talking about." My chest aches. Her mum looks asleep, propped up with three pillows, her lips are dry and chapped. "Well, anyway," Ruby continues, noticing her Mum's lips and putting some balm on from the cupboard by her side. "I wanted you to meet him. We're off to his school prom tonight and I'm his date! I'm wearing that long black dress you bought me for our Christmas party last year and I'm in heels! Me! In heels! I already hate them. Anyway, we need to go now." She waves her hand for me to join her by the bed. I walk over. "Josh is standing by your bed now looking very handsome. He's black curly hair and dimples when he smiles. He's strong, kind, and reliable. Like Dad! And don't tell him I told you," She turns to me. "But I think I'm falling for him." We stare at each other. "She can hear you. The morphine makes her drowsy and it's difficult to keep her eyes open, but she can hear you. I'm sure of it."

"Hi, Mrs Flanagan." My voice croaks and I cough. "Your daughter looks beautiful tonight and I promise to always take good care of her." There's a flicker of her eyelids.

"You best do." I jump as Ruby's dad marches in, smiling. "Now, I've ordered you a taxi to take you and bring you back by eleven. Ruby, can you go and finish the boys' tea before you leave?" She kisses her mum gently on the forehead and I see her mum's eyes flicker once more, she leaves the room whispering something to her dad on the way out. I turn to head out and her dad grabs me gently by the arm, his eyes looking at his wife. "I'll keep it simple. She's very precious to me and if anything should happen to her." He faces me and raises his eyebrows.

"Mr Flanagan. Every day I can't believe why someone as incredible as your daughter would choose to be with someone like me. I promise never to take that for granted."

He pats my back. "Good man." A car beeps its horn outside. "Now go have some fun, she deserves it."

We sit in the back of the taxi holding hands, stealing glances at each other and smiling.

"So, Josh McBride." Ruby turns to face me. "The end is nigh! Reckon you've done enough to pass and get on that joinery course?"

I lean back in the chair. "I don't know." I think back to all the lessons I've struggled in. Lessons where I didn't finish the task and asked to stay back at breaktime and catch up. Lessons where I didn't understand what the task was and daren't ask anyone because it would be obvious how stupid I was. "And if I'm honest," We pass St. Wilfrid's Church. "I don't care."

She playfully taps my leg. "Yes, you do!"

"I don't!" She looks at me doubtfully. "Honestly! I was able to sit down and complete whole exam papers without storming out or giving up. That is enough for me. I don't know whether it was putting a name to how my brain works or people finally listening to me and believing in me." I squeeze her hand. "But maybe for the first time in my whole life, I thought I can do this." She smiles and nods. "Now ... for all we know I might have utterly failed the whole lot of them." She laughs and shakes her head. "But we can cross that bridge when we get to it. I know. I know!" I stress. "I did my best. I'm leaving this school knowing I did my bloody best in those exams."

Ruby smiles and kisses me on the cheek. "Proud of you."

"I'm proud of me too!" I laugh.

The taxi pulls up outside of school and we get out. The outside of school is fizzing with excitement, groups of girls in fancy dresses having their photos taken, boys in oversized suits, teachers dotted around trying to give us freedom but also giving *knowing* looks and checking handbags for alcohol. Ruby holds my hand tight, and I spot a nervous look in her eyes. "I'm right by your side." I reassure her.

"Hey!" Elliot skips over. "Thanks for letting me tag along. I'm not staying long; it was simply to keep my mum happy. She wanted to see me in a suit." He stretches his arms out wide to show off his black suit that he explains his mum ordered from a catalogue.

Ruby hugs him. "You look very dapper." She links arms with us both. "Well, aren't I the lucky one tonight? Two handsome fellas as my date." We follow the excited herd of teenagers into school.

"Freaks!" I turn around and Lewis is swaying behind us,

wearing a T-shirt and jeans with a bottle of beer in his hand. I search for a teacher, but they've all vanished.

"Leave it," Ruby says, grabbing my arm.

"What has become of you, Josh? There used to be a time you were the hard man around school and look at you now. You need a girl to stick up for you and you're best mates with this freak show!" He points at Elliot. "Anyway," he puts the bottle down and it falls over, beer trickling down the pavement. "I thought we could finish what we started the other night." He slurs. Elliot steps forward an inch.

"Go home, Lewis. You're wasted," I state, making sure Elliot and Ruby are behind me.

"Don't get on your high ground now. Your dad was wasted all the time. Oh yeah. Sorry, not your dad. Your dad's in prison," he shouts. "And let's not forget how wasted you were when you jumped in the reservoir!"

My eyes narrow. "What?"

He laughs. "You don't remember, do you?"

Ruby pulls my arm. "Can we go inside? Please?"

I shake Ruby's hand off and step closer to Lewis, choosing my words carefully. "What did you say?"

"That night at the res. Have you ever wondered how you ended up in the water? Freddie had it planned all along as payback for not doing him a favour. He sneaked vodka into your beers, and you didn't even notice! I told you to do what he says. I told you he gets angry if you don't do what he asks. You wouldn't listen so ... splash! In you went! He dared you to jump in and I honestly thought you wouldn't, but you threw yourself right in! Funniest thing I've seen all year, you flapping around like a seal." He laughs.

I step closer. "What's up with you? I could've died."

"Josh!" Ruby shouts.

I clench my fist, take another step. "Elliot could've died."

He doesn't move and our faces are close. He stinks. I glance back to Elliot and Ruby. "Do you know something?"

"What?"

"I feel sorry for you." My voice is low and steady. "Look what I have." I nod back to Ruby and Elliot and back at him. "I've a friend, who thinks that much of me, he jumped into that reservoir to save my life. Who would jump in for you?" His face falls. "And I have a girlfriend who could knock you flat on your face with one punch if I asked her to." I laugh and step back. "Yes, I feel sorry for you. It's not too late to change your ways and you might get someone who gives a damn about you too. Till then, go home and sober the hell up."

I walk away, head high, grabbing Ruby's hand on the way past, just as Marshall appears ushering Lewis off the premises. "All okay, Josh?" he enquires.

I look at Ruby and Elliot. "Yes, Sir. All's fine."

We follow the train of excited students into the school.

"Can you smell that?" Ruby asks.

I sniff my armpits. "What?"

"Not you silly!" She slaps my arm.

"Can you not smell it? The freedom? School's done! We have a long summer ahead. Do you fancy a romantic summer with me? The kind you read about in books. We can go for picnics in fields and ride bikes with baskets on and have the wind in our hair!" She laughs and leans her head on my shoulder. "What do you think?"

I kiss the top of her head. "I think it sounds perfect."

"What about you, Elliot? What are you going to do with yourself before becoming a famous Hollywood star."

"Actually, I've booked a ticket to Paris."

"Paris!"

"Yes, I'm going to visit the Louvre and sit in the gardens there."

"All the way to Paris to see some gardens?" I laugh."Why would you want to do that?"

"Someone told me they're pretty special."

As we enter the school, the band can be heard, and Ruby lets go of my hand and jumps up and down. "It's Overkill! I love this band. They played at our Valentine's Ball last year. Good friends of mine."

She winks at me.

CHAPTER THIRTY-EIGHT

ELLIOT

The school gymnasium has been turned into a magical wonderland thanks to the efforts of Edward and the art committee, the walls are decorated with fairies and stars and a large silver glitter ball spins in the centre of the ceiling. A band has set up on the stage and a handful of brave teenagers are already swaying on the dancefloor. One boy, who I imagine had some *dutch courage* before arriving, does a spectacular knee slide across the dancefloor. There's a buffet along one of the walls, and a table serving non-alcoholic punch and bottles of water. I thought I would feel an utter gooseberry arriving with Josh and Ruby, but it looks like everyone is finding safety in numbers, congregating in small groups around the large hall. Edward walks past with a glass of punch.

"Edward?" Josh shouts. He stops, shocked that Josh McBride's talking to him. "Could you take a picture of us?"

Ruby stands in the middle whilst Edwards takes some pictures. Josh looks my way, "Think it's about time we *are* in some photos." We thank Edward, congratulate him on the decorations and watch him go and ask Maisie, from our history class, to dance. Clare Rogers stands by the buffet, waves, and smiles at me. I wave back.

This is it.

The end of our time at St. Cuthbert's.

I still feel like the scared little boy who arrived in year seven. I search the crowded room and see Felicity enter, wearing a red dress and looking so beautiful I choke on my water. She's with one of her friends and I don't see any sign of a date.

Ruby puts a hand on my back. "Go on! This is your chance. Make it right."

I move forward but Mr Marshall appears. "Elliot." Felicity heads straight onto the dancefloor with her friends. "Can I have a minute?"

"Yes, Sir."

"I wanted to say good luck for the future. You are one of the most naturally gifted students I've ever had the privilege of teaching. A touch more confidence and belief in yourself and you will be unstoppable." I know he means well but highlighting my lack of confidence isn't helping right now. I need to tell Felicity she's the one I want to be with. She's always been the one.

"Thanks, Sir. I'll do my best." We shake hands and he quickly scoots off to the drinks table to smell the punch for any hints of alcohol. I take a seat by the wall and watch the dancefloor fill with students. Josh and Ruby perform silly dances for each other and laugh, head back, mouths open-wide, laughing. They hug, kiss and I doubt they even notice other people in the room. Ruby whispers something in his ear and I watch Josh go up onto the stage and speak to the drummer of Overkill, who then speaks to the lead singer. The music stops and the room erupts into boos. The singer grabs the microphone. "Good evening, St. Cuthbert's!" A loud rapturous applause. "Are we having a good time?" Loud cheers and feet stamping. "Before our next song, we would like to invite a fellow musician up onto the stage to perform an original song of his very own. We've heard he didn't get a chance to sing it at the school talent show, so Elliot Hart, are you out there?"

He puts his hand over his eyes to block out the glare of the spotlights and searches the room.

I freeze.

This can't be happening.

I feel sick.

"Elliot? Come on up!" He hasn't seen me yet. I could sneak through the door behind me and out through the window of the boys' toilets. I could be home and tucked up in my bed with my latest book in thirty minutes.

Claire Rogers catches my eye and points, shouting, "He's here! He's here!" Soon more eyes are on me, clapping and shouting. In a split second, everyone in the room's chanting my name and I stand, legs shaking. I edge around the dancefloor and walk slowly towards the stage, avoiding everyone's gaze, especially trying not to focus on the girl in the red dress. The chanting turns to wild clapping as I step up onto the stage. Josh is smiling ear to ear and gesturing towards the microphone. "Over to you."

I stare at him. "Are you being serious?" He nods. "Hell is filled with people like you, Josh McBride."

He smiles and puts his hands up in mock surrender. "Hey! Ruby's idea! Not mine. Don't shoot the messenger." He jumps off stage to join Ruby who smiles and winks at me. I take my suit jacket off and rest it at the side of the stage. The singer takes his guitar off his shoulders and puts it on mine before leading me to the microphone. The room falls silent, and Felicity's standing in the middle of the dance floor looking like a film star.

"Err ... Hi." The loudness of my voice in the microphone

startles me, I step back, tune in the guitar, and keep my eyes on Felicity. Even though my mouth's dry and I feel like I could throw up, if I don't do this now, then when? "Felicity Hooper," she looks up, untucks her hair from behind her ear to try and hide from the sudden attention. "I've made a few mistakes and recently I've not been very clear with what I wanted to say, and I'm sorry for that, maybe humiliating myself in the next five minutes will make up for it." She looks at me, confused. I take a deep breath and start to strum the strings, moving my fingers effortlessly like Tom taught me. "I've written a few words down ... for you." I strum the strings again.

> Standing in the corridor with your red coat
> and the freckles on your nose,

My voice doesn't sound right. It doesn't sound like when I practised it at home. My hands are shaking and missing the chords. The room's silent. I've been here before. "Sorry, let me try again. False start." I strum the chords again, keeping my eyes on Felicity.

> Standing in the corridor with your red coat
> and the freckles on your nose,
> You make me lost for words,
> You're a star. You're my perfect Nancy,
> You make me lost, you make me, you make me
> lost for words.

The room erupts. I laugh. Everyone's clapping and cheering. Josh and Ruby jump up and down. Felicity looks at me and throws her head back, laughing. My fingers glide over the strings and for the first time since Tom sat with me on his settee and patiently taught me how to play, it feels comfortable. The guitar feels part of me. I stand tall and sing.

> I don't want to be invisible anymore,
> Thank you for making me feel seen,
> What was I waiting for?
> You are, you are, you are the one for me.

More clapping. Felicity's smiling and looking straight at me.

> We're a book club for two. The perfect match.
> You make me lost for words.
> With a scrunch of your nose and the sound of
>   your giggle.
> You make me, you make me, you make me lost
>   for words.

"Go Elliot!" Ruby screams, jumping up and down. "Go on!" She punches the air.

> I don't want to be invisible anymore,
> Thank you for making me feel seen,
> What was I waiting for?
> You are, you are, you are the one for me.

My voice fills every space of the gymnasium.

> Looking pretty hot in my purple cardi,
> You make me lost for words.
> You stood by me from the beginning.
> You make me, you make me, you make me lost
>   for words.

> I don't want to be invisible anymore,
> Thank you for making me feel seen,
> What was I waiting for?
> You are, you are, you are the one for me.

There's a beat behind me as the drummer picks up on the rhythm. Felicity's staring, her hand to her mouth. I sing louder, stand tall, hold the microphone tight. At the last verse, the drummer stops, and I let the guitar hang loosely around my neck. I hold the microphone with both hands, look at Felicity and let the crowd of overexcited teenagers fade away.

> It's time to come clean.
> You are, you are, you are the one for me.

I hold the last note, wait for a moment before the room is suddenly filled with loud clapping, cheering and feet stomping. I wait for the noise to die down. Felicity hasn't moved. She stands still, smiling at me. "Felicity Hooper, you make me lost for words but what I've wanted to say for the last five years is ..." Her eyes grow wider. "Care to dance?" She nods eagerly and there's more clapping. I hand the guitar back, jump off the stage and stride over to her, lift her chin up to mine. "You're the one for me." I softly kiss her lips and move a strand of hair behind her ear. We stop and smile, and I kiss her again. Our arms fold around each other and we pull each other close and kiss again. She pulls aways, studies my face and smiles. "What took you so long, Elliot Hart?"

ACKNOWLEDGMENTS

I did it again! A book does not get to this stage without a lot of support.

Thank you to Jean, Rachel and all the other authors at Creative James Media for your constant support, advice, and enthusiasm. Thanks to Diana for another great cover. A huge thank you to all the teenagers I've come across in my teaching career. You never fail to bring a smile to my face; be it with pride or slight hysteria. A special thank you to those pupils who gave me an insight into dyslexia and how it affects your day-to-day life. I've learnt so much from you.

The Writing Community on Twitter (you know who you are) continue to be the best people to have in your corner! You're such a talented, lovely, and generous bunch of people and it's an absolute pleasure to be on this crazy journey with you all.

There's not a day that passes that I don't feel utterly blessed for the friends in my life. Thank you for always being there for me and making me feel like I can do this. Thank you to Gary, Taps and Ross who freed up their time and read my early 'vomit drafts', giving invaluable feedback. A special mention to Gary and Ang who also lent me their beautiful houses by the sea when a deadline was looming. Thanks to Zoe, my incredibly talented friend and colleague, for creating the much-needed biscuit guide!

Thanks to my dad, when you read my first book in two days and proudly told everyone else to read and review it, my heart could've burst. You're so special to me. To my brothers too, we have been through a lot, and I feel lucky to have you both by my side.

To my husband, Richard. None of my books would be finished without you. Thank you for your constant support and allowing me to sneak writing into our very busy lives. I love you so much.

To my beautiful sons, Sam and Henry. You two are my proudest creations. You're wonderful, kind, funny boys and I feel very lucky to be your mum.

You haven't been able to see me as a real-life author Mum but be rest assured that you're in every character and plot I write. There's not a day that passes that I don't miss you, but I promise to try and be the best I can be because of you. The same goes to you Grandma, my second biggest champion. I miss our cups of tea and chats.

Finally, thanks to anyone who has taken Elliot and Josh into their hearts. They mean a lot to me, and to all the Elliots and Joshs out there? Keep going, look for the kind people, and be proud of making it this far.

ABOUT THE AUTHOR

Kate grew up in a small town in Lancashire, England with her mum, dad and two older brothers. She studied English at Reading University and gained a teaching qualification at Manchester. Nowadays, Kate spends her days teaching English at a local high school in Cheshire and her evenings are spent writing stories close to her heart. She believes teenage years can be particularly difficult and wants to create stories that show empathy and hope for her readers. She lives with her husband, two children and Jessie, the Miniature Schnauzer.

HELPFUL WEBSITES UK

YOUNG CARERS
carersuk.org

GRIEF
thegoodgrieftrust.org

MENTAL HEALTH
youngminds.org.uk

DYSLEXIA
bdadyslexia.org.uk

HELPFUL WEBSITES US

YOUNG CAREGIVERS
apa.org

GRIEF
nacg.org

MENTAL HEALTH
Childrensmentalhealthmatters.org

DYSLEXIA
dyslexiaida.org

Printed in Great Britain
by Amazon